HOME OF THE BEARS
BUILDING OF THE KINGDOM BOOK THREE

R.M ROGERS

Copyright © 2017 by R.M Rogers

All rights reserved.

No part of this book may be reproduced in any form or by any electronic or mechanical means, including information storage and retrieval systems, without written permission from the author, except for the use of brief quotations in a book review.

DEDICATION AND ACKNOWLEDGMENT

Dedicated to Joe, Michael, and the urbane cowboys in my life.

Big thanks to Connie, Gail, Shawna, and the Desert Breeze team.

CHAPTER 1

DENVER

Joanne clipped only the freshest mums from the plants that curved around her front door. Then she went back over every plant, cutting the dead blossoms off. She stood up, her back aching, but she looked with satisfaction at her immaculate front yard. The lawn, a perfect shade of deep green; the neighbor's leaves raked up and bagged, removed forever from her oasis in life — it all looked perfect.

This new neighbor and his new trees did not please Joanne, but she didn't want to start a fight. The neighbor would learn by the fastidious way she had raked up the leaves, and by stacking the bags of leaves out by the mailbox until the trash man came, that she wasn't happy with his new trees and their mess. She would also be a bit cold. She knew how to do that without being obvious. He would want her favor and he would learn to earn it. You don't let leaves blow into her yard without paying a price.

It wasn't as if the leaves didn't have a certain attractiveness at times, with their color contrasting against the deep green of the grass, but she preferred the neat and tidy look. Everyone else in the neighborhood knew that if she had wanted leaves she would have bought and planted trees years ago. The new people would get the message. This was her preferred method of communicating. If the new neighbors didn't get it, she was sure some of the older neighbors would clue them in. *After all, you wouldn't want to live right next door and not be invited to one of Joanne's famous holiday parties.*

She watched as her neighbor across the street walked down his driveway to get his paper. He moved slowly and carefully, having just recovered from a bout with the flu. Joanne waited to see if he saw her. He picked up his newspaper, and as he stood up, they made eye contact and he waved. She waved back. He was a retired judge, and they had known each other for years, although at this moment, she didn't know who the man liked more, her or her ex-husband. Hard to say, and a small knot in her gut formed when she thought about it -- the uncertainty of it all bothered her. She hoped that everyone in this neighborhood sided with her and liked her better, because they knew what she was about.

They knew how hard she had worked on this house, worked on the neighborhood watch program, and how she had always been at their doorstep with a bowl of soup when they were ill. They also knew, they had to know, that her husband had treated her badly. That had to be out there -- that was fact and not even gossip. She waved again at her neighbor and then reentered her house, passed the curving staircase, down the hall to the open kitchen, with the big windows facing the mountains and the immaculate gray and white cabinets and granite counter tops, which included the large island in the center. She retrieved a vase from underneath, recut the flowers and arranged them in the gray, modern-looking vase and put it on the island where her guest liked to perch on the comfortable stool, watch her cook, and admire the view of the Rocky Mountains. The colors were stupendous. Trees were very nice at a distance — especially during the fall. Their warm tapestry of colors could lift anyone's spirits.

She could hear footsteps on the stairs, so she hurried to finish setting a place for him. When he appeared, and settled in on the stool, she smiled and asked, "How about scrambled eggs with this bacon I've cooked?"

"Joanne, you are the best," her cousin Andy said with a big smile as he looked at the draining apple-wood smoked bacon.

She started to pour him a cup of coffee, but he waved her off and poured his own. He sat down again, watching her cook the eggs and admiring the view of the Rocky Mountains.

"You've done this before," he said as he watched her deftly stir the eggs. "Anything you want to talk about?" He knew she needed to talk, but he also knew she probably wouldn't. In her freshly wounded mind, she was a victim, had no responsibility, and she couldn't seem to think or talk any deeper than that, so maybe it was okay if she didn't want to talk. But she did.

"You know, I spent my life helping that man get to where he is, and I took every responsibility seriously. Including cooking eggs and many other things for him and his business associates before and after they went hunting. It was like I ran a hunting lodge. *I helped him get to where he is.*"

"I believe that," said Andy, knowing he had to meet her where she was, and that was all he could do since everything was so painfully fresh in her mind.

"Aren't you eating?" he asked as he dove into the eggs, toast, and bacon. She smiled, shook her head, and sank onto the stool next to him.

"Are you happy with this class? Are you glad you took it?" she asked.

"I am. The class, while a grim topic on suicide, is a necessary one, but I'll also be glad to go home."

"I suppose a lot of the class had to do with drug abuse?"

"Absolutely. We covered a lot of ground. Much of it not pretty. Like I said, I'm ready to go home."

"Missing your kids and wife, are you Pastor Andy? How's that going for you? A new marriage and two teenage kids as part of the bargain. That sounds challenging to me. I'm very happy for you."

"They call me the bald wonder. They are challenging, but I love them. God has blessed me with a family after all. A boy and a girl. Can you believe it? God is so gracious. But, let's talk about you -- you're about to be free of me, and you've had big changes in your life. What's ahead for you, my dear cousin, my almost sister?"

"I can't see very far ahead. I don't want to. I still can't believe it's all happened."

"Okay, how about today?"

"I'm going to spruce up the inside of the house. It will help me think. I was out in the yard this morning. So good for me to get the leaves raked up, and the flowers taken care of every day."

"You love this house. And you have a talent for running a house. I know this is hard. Remember those steps of grief we talked about. And it isn't necessarily a linear process. It takes a while."

She nodded. "It was my life, my career, my hobby, my everything. What can actually be more important than a house, a home? Where people learn to connect, nurture each other. Where people can rest from the world, pursue their own interests. I always thought it was an important job. I enjoyed watching my husband succeed. I felt the same about our daughter."

Andy watched her eyes cloud with memories and sadness, but he decided to say nothing.

"And I valued the work at the church. I did good work and the pastors often told me so. Now, I don't even want to go. I wonder what those people think of me? All that work at the church, events I had here in my home for the church — all of that took work, and now, my whole life looks like a sham."

"I know it's painful," said Andy, but he could tell she didn't hear him.

"Do you want to know the worst of it?"

Joanne used that phrase a lot, but Andy didn't say that. He let her continue.

"The worst of it is, it's not as if I got dumped for a younger woman, or anything like that. She might be older than me. I think she plays golf and people who have met her seem to like her. They aren't afraid to tell me that. Someone said the other day that she has a good sense of humor."

He knew they were on touchy and likely unproductive territory, but he had to ask. "What has Jasmine said about her?"

"Well, first of all, she doesn't answer any questions. You would think, being my only daughter and considering everything that she would answer some questions, but she doesn't. That really irks me."

Andy reached out and took her hand. "I want you to think about something. I want you to go to Washington State with me and get out of here for a while." *There, I've finally said it. The whole idea has been scary, but it seemed like the Holy Spirit had put it in my mind, and so there it is, out in the open.*

"What would I do? It may be sad here, but at least I know what I'm about. I can't believe you would suggest such a thing."

"I can help with that. Hear me out."

"I don't think so! You're a traveling pastor! With six churches, up and down the coast and in the islands, and a new wife and kids; I don't think you'll have any time for me at all."

"That may likely be true, but here's the thing. I'm about to add a seventh church in a lovely little town in the middle of the mountains. A town named Crystal. And I need your help."

"Oh, please. What could I do for you there?"

"There's this old Victorian house that has been donated. The elderly couple who had lived there came from logging families, so the house has quite a history. They wanted to donate it as a church after they had both died, and so they have. I'm thinking it will be my home base once our two teenage kids have left the nest, but it really needs to be spruced up and evaluated for repairs. I'd like to have it habitable for the Christmas festivities and my family by Thanksgiving. Actually, my friends in New Mexico, Collin and Julie, they've been talking about coming for Thanksgiving. I think it would be grand to have a large Thanksgiving dinner there, a big family event, before we open as a church. We have friends there that I would want to welcome before they even have to consider it being a church."

Lord, what is she thinking? Her world has turned upside down and I don't blame her for being grief-stricken. But I could use the help, and I know how you are, Lord. You like to develop situations beyond anything we can imagine. Sometimes we see ourselves better in a new situation. Andy took a sip of coffee. Joanne didn't say anything, so he continued.

"I think it would be grand for you to stay through Thanksgiving and meet some of these people. They have lived interesting lives and walked through a lot with me. One of the people I want you to meet is a young man named Tyler. He has only one arm and he's skittish about church. He and I go way back. He and his wife have the cutest little girl. And there are others, like my friends Julie and Collin, that I just mentioned. You'll like Julie; she's an accomplished artist. What do you say? Will you at least think about it?"

"I can think about it, but I'm not promising anything. I have plenty to do here."

Andy watched her restless eyes, and knew she was tied up in knots. He took her hand in his. "Give me some credit for knowing something about these situations. This could be the exact right thing to do. Give yourself a change of scenery and come out west with me for a few weeks. You would be helping me out more than I can say." She would say no, he was sure of it, but it would be such a good thing. On several levels.

"Are you out of your mind? I love you, but think of it. Jasmine might need me. This house needs what it needs."

Oh, Lord, help me say the right things here, and then help me let go of the outcome. I know I cannot afford to get twisted up in her thinking.

"Do you remember those two years when you lived with us? When your mother was sick?" asked Andy.

"Of course."

"You were frightened. You didn't know if your mother would live, if your dad was going to take care of both of you. But you slowly got to trust me and my family. You slowly got to relax. You even got to where you could play some pranks on me, although I will always take pride in teaching you the fine art of pranks on others."

She smiled, softening at the memories. "You were a handful," said Joanne. "I couldn't believe what you got away with. You had no sisters or brothers, and you drove your parents nuts, but they still loved you. And me."

"Joanne, you are quite a capable woman and your life isn't over yet. You've been through a lot of hardship and heartbreak. But I still ask you to trust me. I'm thinking this would be really good for you. I would also benefit from it. See if you can trust me again. Even if it seems like a bad idea. Even if you are mad at God and don't want to trust anybody, see if you can trust me in this."

"I'll think about it, you are so very kind to ask me. I appreciate the offer."

"Cut the diplomatic society talk. I know you. We'll talk later. Think it over."

"Andy, I hope you know how much I appreciate your being here with me during this time. I never dreamed my life would turn out this way. All those expectations when I got married, all the joy put into this house, all that has ended up like this. Unbelievable, the humiliation of it all. I don't know what I would have done without you. But I can manage now. I will manage now."

Andy rinsed off his dishes and put them in the dishwasher while Joanne sat quietly staring out the window. He took her hands in his and prayed for both of them, their day, and specifically the work each of them had to do that day. He then kissed her on the cheek, collected his books, stuffed them in his backpack, and he drove off to his class knowing two things. First, he knew it would be difficult for her to accept his invitation. Second, he knew even before he had driven out of the circular driveway that she was back to cleaning and trying to make everything perfect. She couldn't fix the past, however, by making that house perfect now.

∼

After Andy left, Joanne cleaned up the kitchen, cherishing every beautiful surface, cleaning and polishing until she knew that she was obsessing and avoiding the rest of the house.

She wandered back into the hallway, stopping to look at herself in the large framed mirror. Who was that woman? She still looked slim, but that was only because she knew better than to wear tight clothing. Her hair, the same style as she had worn through the years, a bob, just above her shoulders. Gray, now, but the same. Her skin looked good, but she was older and there was only so much cosmetics and collagen supplements could do. It frightened her to look at herself, to see herself as an older, single woman. She moved on to the living room, standing at the wide entrance, admiring the fireplace, the hardwood floors — not laminate but wide maple planks. The silk rug in the center, with the leather sofas on three sides, and the coffee table, made of maple burl and big and all from one slice of a tree. A monumental tree. The horror of something wrong gripped her, but she didn't know what it was. She slowly scanned the room and asked herself, *what is wrong here? Something doesn't smell right. It's faint, but something isn't right.*

The paintings on the walls hung straight, the pillows on the sofas, the dining room table at the end — all looked fine, but that smell. What was it? She moved around the room, trying to figure it out but stopped at the credenza by the dining room table — that was it. She saw it immediately as she peered into the large candle holder and saw a cigarette stub, snuffed out, but sitting there creating its own tawdry smell. How long it had been there, she didn't know. Maybe one of several repairmen who had been around in the last couple of days cleaning the fireplace had left it there. Maybe it had been there longer and she had just been so overcome with the reality of the divorce proceedings that she hadn't noticed. Whatever. She was past it all now. Now she would get back on top of her game and she would go forward, with God's help she would go forward. And that meant disposing of the cigarette stub.

After doing that, she went through the rest of the main floor, even, opening the doors to the library, formerly known as her husband's office. She stood at the pocket door and looked around. There remained no evidence of him. Over the last few months, after he had moved out, she had slowly put her own things in the room. The desk, a lady-like replacement for his masculine monolithic desk, and the lights and the bookcases all looked warm, tasteful, and feminine. She had not, however, used it. It looked good, but she preferred to sit in the kitchen to tend to any business she needed to take care of. She had been afraid of this room before, but now, seeing it, and knowing he would not somehow emerge to say something horrible to her, she felt relieved and left the doors open and the light on. There was something cheerful about it. Something fresh, dynamic, and cheerful. Using it didn't cross her mind, but leaving the lights on and the doors open seemed like the right thing.

What she needed to do now was look at the spaces that Jasmine had called her very own, but first, she poured herself a cup of coffee. *Jasmine, my pride and joy, you are my one and only child, I miss you so much.* Jasmine had left home for her freshmen year of college and had not come back for the divorce proceedings. Joanne missed her daughter's companionship, but she knew it was the right thing for Jasmine to stay at school and forge ahead. Now, however, the divorce was final and even Joanne needed to move ahead, and that meant get the house in order and ready to sell.

Joanne knew she was stalling. She rinsed out her coffee cup, took a deep breath, and resolutely walked out of the kitchen.

Joanne stood at the top of the basement stairs, filled with memories. Jasmine's domain. *Jasmine and her friends lived, studied, laughed, watched movies, and watched the news, ever ready to learn, criticize, and mimic when they felt especially witty. They had been funny, when they decided to mimic certain politicians or celebrities. Jasmine and her friends made me laugh and feel young, and now that was gone. Forever? The quiet house had no laughter in it this day.*

Joanne walked down the carpeted steps into the basement, aware of the silence, her own steps making hardly a sound. She looked around the large room. It looked like Jasmine and her friends had just left and that they might return at any moment. Magazines, DVDs, and CDs, lay around instead of being put back on a shelf in an orderly manner. Joanne picked up sports magazines and flipped through them before she stacked them on the shelf. Jasmine loved sports. She played tennis; she liked rowing. Joanne ran her hand around the edge of the pool table and then the foosball table and then the poker table. No dormitory would have all this. Would she miss any of this, living in a dorm room with another girl? Didn't she give her daughter everything that could help her grow up, including a place to be with her friends? A place of privacy, fun, food, and security from a large and dangerous world? Jasmine could have decided to go to a university in Denver, but no, she had to go to school in Colorado Springs and her dad agreed.

I don't want to be here this day. I can't do this. This was enough for this day, this was all she could handle of the room that Jasmine and her friends lived in, did homework in, worked on school plays in. This was all she could handle. It was time to go upstairs and see, really look, at Jasmine's bedroom. Joanne's heart felt heavy and painful as she left the basement. It was like Jasmine was still there but yet she wasn't.

As she reached the main floor, which she had just dealt with only a few minutes before, it seemed oppressive to her, and she moved with speed to avoid it and get up the stairs to the third level, but as she started up the stairs to the bedrooms, the front doorbell rang.

Reluctantly, Joanne looked through the peep hole. Bev, the real estate agent from down the street. She was Larry's pick, not hers. *No. I just won't open the door. No, I can't do that; my car is out front. She knows I'm here.* Joanne opened the door, but not all the way.

"Hi, Joanne! I was hoping you were home. Sorry I didn't call first. But your ex called me last night and he said it would be okay for me to come by today." Bev smiled. A smirk actually.

Joanne opened the door a little more. Joanne wasn't tall, but she looked down at Bev, shorter, plump, and her short hair nothing like Joanne's carefully curved under bob. In fact, her hair stood straight up. An attempt, no doubt, to look younger.

"Look, Bev, this isn't a good day for me to show you the house. Why not next week? That would be better for me."

"It would just take a few minutes to take a preliminary look around. You can let me do that, can't you?" Bev said brightly. She said it as if it were a question, but Joanne knew better.

Joanne knew her ex-husband wouldn't think of calling her and discussing it with her, or even giving her a warning. "Now probably isn't a good time. I've just started cleaning. And you know, we haven't actually decided what to do."

Bev didn't hesitate. "I know you have a lot on your mind, but your ex is expecting me to call back with an assessment, and I've got to visit my sick mother today. Truly, I won't be in your way."

There's that smile again. I'd like to smack her in the teeth. Joanne didn't have the will or the strength to argue. And besides, what would the neighbors think? She opened the door and let Bev in.

"I'll be upstairs. Wander at will." She didn't mean that, but it sounded good. Bev marched toward the kitchen and Joanne laboriously went up the stairs. Joanne stood at the doorway of her daughter's room and looked around. She couldn't bear to look at it but she couldn't bear to leave, either. Where should she start? Her feet felt like lead. The bulletin board still had her high school graduation pictures on it, and the blue and gold striped comforter was casually thrown across the bed as if Jasmine had been in a hurry, that very morning.

She started on her left and decided to strip the bed. She was half way through when Bev appeared at the door.

"The house is immaculate. Great shape. And great floor plan. Except in here. But kids are kids." Bev took in the messy bookshelves, the stack of old stuffed toys in the corner.

Joanne wouldn't tolerate Bev standing there, seeing her daughter's room, and criticizing her child and therefore herself.

"I have work to do!" Joanne said, hoping that Bev would get the signal and leave, but not to be. As Joanne continued with the bed, Bev marched in, opened the door to the bathroom, and looked in.

"I haven't had time to clean in there," said Joanne.

Bev came out and then opened the closet door, looked around, and then checked out the view from the window.

Leave, now, *or I'll scream*, thought Joanne, as she continued to strip the bed.

Bev said, "It's amazing how helpless I perceived my kids to be. Just amazing. And, when they each left, I couldn't imagine that they were getting on without me."

While Bev carried on about her kids and what they were doing in college, Joanne pretended to listen while she continued to strip the bed, but a plan formulated in her mind. She would go see Jasmine at school. What a perfectly lovely idea. It was certainly time to go visit Jasmine, and she now had the perfect excuse. She herself would go through every part of this room, and collect things that she knew Jasmine would want at college, things that Jasmine had forgotten to take, or things that she didn't know she would need and be too proud to ask. She would figure it all out and Jasmine would love her for it.

"I have a potential buyer coming into town soon, and I think this house would be perfect. I'll talk to your ex tonight." Bev turned and left without saying another word.

Joanne sat back down on the bed and dissolved into tears. How rude of that woman, to come in here and say what she did and do what she did. How rude. How cruel even.

Joanne picked up the sheets and took them to the laundry room at the end of the hall. After starting the machine, she decided to go back outside. The fresh air and the fall day -- that would get rid of the unease she felt in the house. All the memories, the rawness of the recent wounds, and then the real estate agent rubbing salt into it all. Joanne had endured enough this day, and she couldn't stand one more minute of the pain. The flowers and the fresh air would help. She could only take on the house one little step at a time.

J asmine left the college campus and walked briskly down the busy boulevard. *I hate my parents. They couldn't keep their marriage together, they could not be authentic people, and I am ready to be separate and different.*

Not only that, here I am in this college, and granted it was the college of my choice, but still. I am here without a car. With all the craziness in the world, with all their craziness, why am I here in this college, without a car? What were they thinking? I have had my own car since I was sixteen, and now they don't want me to have a car. Unreal.

Jasmine walked along the sidewalk, grateful for its safety as a pickup raced down the road, spattering puddles of rain. She hoped that no one saw her. She had not yet made any strong relationships and the ones she had were new and untried. They were likely to not be impressed with her and her prospects at the college to see her walking along in the rain. She pulled her hood further over her head and kept going.

When Jasmine got to the shopping center, she turned in and found shelter in the strip mall. It wasn't a regular mall, of course, but it had enough to help her out this day, and her first effort was the health food store, where she could get the tea that she liked. Jasmine took refuge among the shelves of pretty kitchen items, the cosmetics, and all the food. What she really needed was just the tea, but she actually wanted the cream for her feet, and when she finished, she felt better. She wandered down the sidewalk, looking into the windows, the kitchen store, the businesses, and came to a unique shoe store.

She went in, feeling comforted by the fragrance of good leather and the displays of stylish shoes. *How lucky to have found this.*

By the time she left the store, she had a shoe box to carry, and she felt even better. The boots were actually booties, but would be perfect to wear around campus and going to class. The big store on the strip mall was a discount store — not one of Jasmine's favorite places to shop, but, she was going in anyway.

Not as comforting as a big pretty department store, but it was out of the weather and worth a look. Jasmine started at the jewelry counter and breezed through the men's department. The toys didn't interest her, nor did the kitchenware section. No dorm room needed the housewares items, but when she got to lady's shoes, she took her time to see what was there. The same with lingerie, and women's clothes.

Nothing interested her until she got to women's jackets, and she started looking through her size when four other girls showed up, laughing and talking, also interested in the jackets.

"Heh," one of them said, looking at Jasmine. "Aren't you in my English class?"

"Yeah, I recognize you," said Jasmine. "I like our professor. He's cool."

"I suppose so, but I find the class a bit boring. What about these jackets — a great price, aren't they?"

Jasmine agreed, and they kept looking, talking about their English class, and then another girl mentioned they were going to eat Italian food at the restaurant next door. She invited Jasmine to join them.

"Sure, I'd love to." Jasmine's mood brightened even more. The day was improving by the hour. She decided to buy a jacket, a red jacket that would match the red boots she just bought. After she finished the purchase, she waited for the other girls at the door, so happy to be included.

The five girls entered the cheerful Italian restaurant, and Jasmine inhaled the heavenly fragrance of pizza and slow-cooked spaghetti sauce. They got a booth and continued talking, mainly about a dance they were going to that weekend, and what they would wear. None of them were part of the hiking club that was Jasmine's main interest outside of class.

They politely asked her if she was going to the dance.

"No, don't have a date. Don't dance that well anyway."

Two of them looked knowingly at each other, nodded, and then the blond with the kind face, said, "We know someone, like he's my brother, actually. We could set you up with him. He's pretty cute. For a brother."

"Oh, what a sweet thing," said Jasmine. "But I don't think so."

"Oh, come on. He's easy to get along with. A bit of a dork, but you could meet some other guys that way."

"No, really. I'm just not up to any dates right now. I'm doing well to just get used to my classes. But thanks anyway."

They took that well enough. Jasmine didn't tell them that her family had just split apart, her childhood home was likely to be sold, and she was in college without a car, and a date was just not looking like anything of interest to her. What if her parents sold the house and she never saw it again? What if her dad moved away and she never saw him again? There was another woman, she knew that. How did he justify that, especially since he had been an elder in the church? Jasmine shut down the chatter in her head and concentrated on listening to the other girls. She felt rejuvenated, but afraid. Afraid of the future, afraid of how to carry on her life, and afraid of what her parents would do next, but these girls didn't need to know all that. She felt better for shopping and for the happy energy of these girls.

Jasmine paid her share of the bill and then said goodbye at the door. The rain steadily beat on the asphalt parking lot, the cars, and the eave over the sidewalk. Jasmine watched the girls head off in different directions. If some of them were going back to the college, Jasmine didn't know it, and she wouldn't ask them for a ride, anyway.

She pulled out her umbrella and unclasped it. Her packages, more than she had intended to buy, she carried awkwardly under her arm. She started off with the umbrella held high, leaving behind the solace of the stores, their pretty merchandise, and the girls who chattered happily about their weekend plans. Jasmine marched resolutely back to the college, hoping that none of those girls saw her walking.

CHAPTER 2

LAS VEGAS

Waiting to go back out on stage, Dennis didn't think he could do it. Not one more time. He was through with it all even if the money had been extraordinarily good. He was a wealthy man, after all and he needed a change and deserved a change. He had certainly managed his money well and didn't need to work again, ever.

He remembered what he had in his pocket, popped the pill into his mouth, drank out of the nearest water bottle, and waited. He could feel his mood lifting.

He heard the announcer, he heard the crowd roaring, seeming to lift the ceiling. He could see Lance in the shadows on the other side of the stage. Lance nodded at him and Dennis and the band entered from stage left. The crowd cheered and the music began. Then the crowd started chanting, "Lance! Lance! Lance!" and before he emerged, they could hear his familiar unmistakable notes on his guitar, and then Lance entered from stage right. The crowd, which had been loud before, now went berserk.

They played all their hit songs. Over twenty albums of best sellers and they played some of Lance's favorites, even though they weren't best sellers. They took only a quick break and then played more, and the crowd, caught up in the music and knowing what Lance was going through, kept building enthusiasm.

Dennis started the last set with a vigor he didn't feel in his heart. He looked down at the young women surrounding the stage, their mouths open, waving their arms. He knew what they wanted, and knew a fair amount of their attention could be for him, but all he felt for them as he played on was indifference at best, but more like disdain. He'd had plenty of what they had offered, and had it for years, and now it no longer tempted him. He knew, many times, that the women were married and had no qualms about what they were doing. And he hadn't thought about it much, but now, whether they were married or not, they disgusted him. His wife Sally had helped him find a new life, a new way of seeing things, and he felt safe in her arms. He didn't need any other women. He and Sally would spend the rest of their lives together.

Dennis thought about Sally as he played on, watching Lance, and knowing and doing what Lance liked. Sally, tan, fit, brown eyes and brown hair, the love of his life. He had met her in a rehab center. She had faced drugs, violent men, and her own less-than-great thinking. She thought about the principles she had learned in the rehab center and she had changed her life. She had been through hell and back and she loved him. How could he be so lucky? She deserved the best he could give her, and that would never be enough. He needed to quit thinking about Sally and focus on Lance and this crowd. Crowds like this always needed to be watched. Never totally ignore them or something could go wrong, very fast.

Focus, focus. Focus on the music, on Lance, and keep your eye on the crowd. Get this done, and then you are through. Focus on the music. Do it for Lance, do it for Sally, and get it done well.

Dennis felt the sweat trickling down his face, he felt the rhythm of the music throbbing in his body, and the power in his hands and arms as the music built to a crescendo. He watched the lead singer and kept the pace, helped him build until the crowd of thirty-somethings was whipped into ecstasy, and then it was over, the last notes reverberating through the floors and the walls.

They bowed, but there was no encore. Dennis knew how bad Lance was feeling. So did the crowd. They knew Lance was sick and they knew this was the last time, and they could yell and scream but there would not be an encore. They knew Lance and the band had given their all, and had nothing left to expend.

Backstage, he put his arm around Lance. "Is there anything I can do?" asked Dennis.

"Tell the guys if they need me, to come by tomorrow, but after that I'm in surgery. I need to get this surgery done and be onto recovery."

Dennis hugged him, knowing that Lance's optimism was ill-founded. Lance clung to him. They both knew the truth, but had kept a positive face for everyone. Dennis grabbed Lance by the shoulders and looked directly into his eyes.

"I love you, man."

"I know. You're a good friend. We've walked through a lot together. You'll be by tomorrow?" asked Lance

"Sure. Got to at least pick up my money."

Lance laughed. "I've got to say, you've never put the money first, and I appreciate that."

"I'll be around tomorrow, and I'll drive you to the hospital."

Dennis went back to the platform and from the side he could see the crowd clamoring for them to come back out. He could see the women. He felt sorry for them, but there was nothing he could do. Tomorrow he would help Lance as best he could, get his money, and then he had a different life planned. He wanted different things. It was time to call his mother and his wife. It was time to give Sally, and yes, even Ellen, his mother, the life they needed and had so patiently waited for. They had been good sports, but now it was their turn. What they wanted, he also wanted.

∼

The next day, Dennis waited at the side door for the valet to bring his car around, and despite the seriousness of the day, he took great pleasure in thinking about his Rolls Royce. He had done well, and he owed it all to Lance. Lance, who had already made it big in the music world, Lance, who many years ago, came into the bar where Dennis and his band were playing, and sat there listening all night. If anyone had recognized him, they didn't show it. They gave Lance his privacy, and respected the two men who sat with him, looking very big and business-like.

That night Lance stayed through the whole evening, and when the band played their last number, Lance approached him, not the rest of the band, but him, and asked him to sit down and talk with him. That was the biggest moment of his life. He accepted Lance's offer on the spot, and life changed.

The silver Rolls came out of the parking garage and Dennis smiled. His pride and joy. A symbol of his success in life. The beautiful machine eased up the drive and stopped. Dennis tipped the valet, listened to the young man's comments about the car, smiled, and then got in. Time to walk Lance through the day.

Later in the hospital, it was Lance, Lance's sister, and Dennis staring at the bed and the hospital gown laid out for him. "I'm not going to stay here and watch my brother get naked," the sister said.

"How about a hug?" Lance asked her.

"No. I don't want to touch you and risk germs. You know I love you." She turned and left the room. Dennis saw her tears.

"Guess I'll follow her. I don't like looking at naked men," said Dennis. "And you know how I feel about you."

"Do you think there's life after death?" asked Lance, looking pensive.

This is not the time to ask that, thought Dennis. *Not here at the last minute.*

"Of course, I do. But it's too soon for you to be going there. You're going to be just fine."

Lance nodded and waved Dennis away.

Dennis went back to the waiting room and sat down by the sister. She looked grave. Older than Lance, not musically inclined, and very protective of her little brother, she exemplified the perfect big sister.

"Do you believe in miracles?" she asked Dennis.

"I think sometimes that's what happens, miracles. God does them once in a while."

"So you believe in God?" She shook her head. "I just don't go there. I can't get my head around the whole God thing. Especially when there's so much bad stuff around."

Dennis didn't respond. He thought this was once again a little late in the game to be talking about whether or not God existed.

She fell silent, and then started thumbing through a magazine without looking at the pages. Dennis just waited. He didn't want to read, or pretend to read. He didn't want to get some food, like the nurse recommended. She said it would be a long surgery and she would call him when there was news. He got up and got a cup of water from the dispenser and sat back down. He was committed. He would stay as close to Lance as he could. He would do everything he could to walk this path with Lance. He owed everything to Lance and he would be loyal and focused on this day. The waiting, the quietness plodded on. The press and everyone else were kept on the first-floor reception room of the hospital. Privacy for the darling of the music world. The man who gave hope through his music.

Dennis saw the doctor's feet before he saw the man. He must have fallen asleep, because he took a moment to focus on the feet and then look up and see the doctor. Dennis knew by the doctor's face it was over. A worthy try, but it was over.

Lance's sister dissolved into tears and fell into Dennis's arms. They stood, holding each other, and cried until they could cry no more. *So this is sad, so very sad, because this is all the family this man had,* thought Dennis. *Me, his lead guitarist, and his sister. A man ought to have more family than this.*

The sister was taken back to say goodbye to Lance, and Dennis called Lance's publicist/spokesman.

"He's gone," said Dennis. "Odds were against him, and he lost."

"I'll take care of everything. A security agent will be up there to escort you both out of the building, away from the press. I've got it from here. I'm sorry. You were very close to him."

Lance's sister wanted to stay with the body, so Dennis, with the security guard, exited the building from the rear executive elevator down to the parking lot. There, once again was his Rolls Royce. He drove it to the hotel where they had so recently played their last concert. He checked for any personal belongings and walked in. He found the woman he was looking for in her office on the second floor.

"My goodness, Dennis. You've been through a lot today. I just heard on the news. What can I do for you?"

"You've taken good care of us while we were here. You took good care of Lance especially. Thank you for that."

"You're welcome. Glad to. Sorry you've had such a rough day."

"Not as rough as many of yours, I'll bet. Besides booking the shows, you fill in as a waitress. That takes guts. I also know you have a special needs child at home, too."

"I do what I need to do to pay the bills."

"I appreciate that, and so I'd like to give you this." He handed her the keys to his Rolls.

"What's this?" she asked.

"It's down in the parking lot. The valet knows which one."

Stunned, the woman stood up, walked around her desk, and gave Dennis a hug. "You are the nicest man. I can't believe you would do this. I know you love that car!"

"I do, but I'm ready to have another car. I think you will no doubt sell it, but give yourself a thrill in it a couple of times before you do that."

"I will. You have just made our lives so much easier!"

He smiled as he walked out of the building. *I'll like remembering the look on her face for the rest of my life.*

∾

Ellen, Dennis's mother, and Sally, his wife, were tired of waiting, tired of living together in the small apartment outside of Las Vegas, and tired of the relentless sun.

Ellen looked at herself in the mirror. Not bad looking for early sixties. She jogged, she hiked, she lifted weights. Her gray hair told her age, but that didn't bother her. She would not dye it, but wore it in a short bob or pony tail. The sun, however, the Nevada sun was drying her up, and that bothered Ellen. Her skin was turning leathery and dry.

Soon it would be time to leave and she waited anxiously every day for the phone call that would change their lives. Otherwise, she was doomed to alligator skin. And she needed some space between her and her daughter-in-law, Sally. Not that she didn't like Sally, but they weren't meant to live together for long periods. A smart girl, and she had a sense of humor, but neither her son nor her daughter-in-law could think like she could, and she aimed to keep both of them on track and focused. That's what she had done with her son, and she had not lost that role when Dennis and Sally got married. Sally adored Dennis, and followed her mother-in-law's direction. What more could a mother want? It was close to time, however, and she was ready for the plan to move forward and she was ready for a little space.

Her daughter-in-law, Sally, peered at her from down the hallway.

"Did you get stuck in the hallway, mesmerized by yourself in the mirror?" asked Sally.

Her daughter-in-law did have a sense of humor. She was also quite adventurous, and Ellen liked that — they got along well, considering it could be worse. They both loved the same man, Ellen's son, Dennis.

"I suppose so. Frightening to see what this desert air does to my skin."

"I know. Soon we will not be so dependent on cosmetics to save our skin."

Sally was good-looking and Ellen liked that for her son. She knew how he was. Sally would also be faithful to him. She could see that from the beginning. That meant a lot to her, too. They both had to be led, they weren't as smart as she was, but they would all benefit. They recognized that. The world, science, and how things worked -- Ellen knew more than these two, and they trusted her.

Ellen returned to the kitchen and peered at her rock collection and her mushroom growing experiment, which took up one half of the kitchen counter. Mushrooms were the strangest plants on the planet, with the most secrets and possible use in the future. She never tired of their mysteries, and their shapes, and their colors.

"I need more test tubes," Ellen said.

"But you will dump all those experiments once we leave, won't you? Why bother at this point?" asked Sally.

"Right," said Ellen. "*I will be optimistic* and assume I won't need more test tubes for some time. No way to take them along. But I'll take the rocks and minerals. I just hope we get the phone call soon. It has to be soon. Lance is dead, after all.

"What about all these pictures?" asked Ellen as she stared up at the pictures taped on the kitchen cabinets.

"I think the pictures won't go with us. After all, they were taken by somebody else. We will have our own pictures."

Just then the phone rang. Ellen stood there while she listened to Sally answer the phone. It was their man. She tried to not listen, but she couldn't help it. The apartment was small. They sounded focused. Happy. Dennis was tired. All good.

Sally got off the phone and smiled at Ellen. "Yahoo and hot damn! We are headed to Washington State! Let's go get those art supplies, because we leave in the morning! We leave the sun behind!"

Ellen threw her arms up in the air, and then grabbed Sally, almost dancing out the door.

"Are you ready?" she asked Sally. "Are you ready for the rest of your life?"

"I'm ready and willing. And willing to leave this desert. I'm ready for what I know, and that's boats and water and good times!"

"I'm ready, too. I'm sorry to be so happy so soon after Lance has died, but Lance would want us to carry on." Ellen smiled at her daughter-in-law, hoping she didn't seem too callous to Sally. *My son and his wife are moving along. We are all ready for a change. It is time to take a chance and have more in life. I need to go shopping and then spend the rest of the day writing up my rock and mineral studies. Yes, indeed. It was time to take chances, explore life, and get out of this sun. And dump the mushroom growing experiments.*

"Too bad about Lance, but it was his time," said Sally. "He certainly had a large life. He died young, but he lived large. No need to cry over that. I didn't really understand Dennis's somber attachment to Lance. It amounted to a sentimentality that I couldn't relate to. Maybe I was a bit jealous of their relationship?"

"Don't worry about it," said Ellen. "Dennis was totally committed to Lance, but it wasn't even a real brotherly love. It wasn't as if Dennis actually loved Lance. I know what love is, and they really didn't. Not the way real brothers love each other. I don't have time to be sentimental over Lance. It is time to *live*."

∼

DENVER

Back in Jasmine's room, Joanne felt a knot of worry in her stomach. Jasmine should have taken these shoes; Jasmine should have taken these basic books, like her Bible, the dictionary, and the daily devotional book. What was Jasmine thinking? Joanne went into the bathroom, and was horrified at what her daughter had not taken. Here was the special anti- sun cream that Joanne had bought for her, and look at this, a whole box of lip balm. Joanne continued on, wondering about her daughter's judgment, saying to herself Jasmine needs this, and that and the last straw was her wrist brace for playing tennis. There it was, lying in plain sight in the top drawer in the bathroom. The doctor had said she would always need to wear it, probably for the rest of her life.

That sealed it; that made a trip necessary. A box full of things was good enough, and the wrist brace made it mandatory. No discussion. Of course her mind was full of a jumble of things she needed to do, but a part of her was at peace in knowing she needed to go visit her daughter. This would be a priority. This would make her feel better. Her daughter always made her feel better. She felt good about the day's accomplishments and that particular decision. And then the phone rang. Her now ex-husband. Larry.

She picked up the phone, hoping he had some comfort for her in these strange days that she was trying to navigate by herself, but his tone just in saying hello was no comfort. He continued -- berating her for not signing up with the real estate agent.

"Stop, stop," she said. "You and I have other things to talk about."

"What is it? What?"

"Like we have a daughter and we are still her parents."

No response.

"Are you there? Did you hear what I said?"

"Joanne, have you totally lost it? I figured you would go bonkers with her gone to school and the divorce, but really -- what is the problem?"

"Well, *thank you for caring*. I did find some things I thought she forgot, including her wrist brace. And I get no appreciation from you for that or how much I am doing to take care of this house."

"You are right, Joanne. I apologize. Just call her or take it down there. There is no emergency. I'm surprised you hadn't made up an excuse to go see her before this."

"*What's that supposed to mean*? How dare you? At least I was available to her, while you were out doing whatever."

"Like earning a living, so that you and our daughter could live well, buy nice clothes, and now she can have a great education at a private college."

"Of course, you don't mention your *extracurricular* activities."

"Look, Joanne. I've got to go. Please sign up with the realtor. And either mail the stuff to Jasmine or go see her. It's what your best at, waiting on her."

Joanne frosted up, but he ended the conversation. She sat down on her daughter's bed and tried to breathe. For the second time in two days, Joanne was so mad she couldn't speak. Where had her life gone? Dedicated to her marriage, her child, her home, she had worked hard, and hadn't it all worked out well? The house was beautiful, bought at a good price, nurtured, kept updated, and used for entertaining her husband's business associates.

The house had nurtured their daughter as she grew up, a happy toddler, a searching smart child, a growing teenager. All through the stages of growing up, the house, especially Jasmine's room, had changed with her and nurtured her.

And what about the community? Neighborhood parties, church meetings, and Bible studies. The house had served, and served well. And now her ex-husband expected her to just get rid of it and get the money out of it so they could split that. Now he expected her to move on as fast as he had, but she couldn't. She just couldn't.

Where was Andy? They had a little time left. Maybe he could help her.

No. No, no, no. She didn't need Andy. She didn't need to consult with anybody. She needed to get ready. She was an adult and she could now make her own decisions about her own life. She would get herself ready. Probably not call Jasmine too much ahead of time. They would be so glad to see each other. All the planning would occur spontaneously and the joy of anticipating it made her giddy. The pain of the phone call and all that had happened these last few months was already subsiding. Yes, Jasmine always had a way of taking the sting out of her life. Jasmine had always been that way.

CHAPTER 3

It was Saturday morning, and Joanne frantically looked for something to wear. What do you wear to a college? How do you look tasteful and motherly and not over-the-hill, all at the same time? Jeans and her sweater — the best she could do. She ate a frozen waffle and headed out the door.

She drove from north Denver and headed down to Colorado Springs to see her daughter. She had lost everything dear to her, but not her daughter, other than a natural progression to college. She deserved this short trip, after everything she had been through. The traffic was light after she left Denver, and her thoughts drifted.

They had always been close; she could tell her daughter so much that she couldn't say to anyone else. Joanne knew she needed that again. Sure, Jasmine needed her own life, and the divorce had been hard on her, but Joanne knew they needed each other. The truth was, she had spent her whole adult life taking care of her husband and then her daughter and she could not imagine life alone. It was too painful to be alone and it couldn't be right. On a day-to-day basis she was not special to anyone, and she could not imagine what life was going to be like. If Andy hadn't been there, she didn't know what would have become of her, but he was leaving tomorrow. Life looked bleak and frightening. She was, to use a current phrase that she liked, taking care of herself, by driving to reconnect with her daughter.

She had her box of things for Jasmine, especially the wrist brace. The truth was, she couldn't remember anything else she had put in the box, but no matter. The main thing was they would reconnect.

I've called Jasmine twice, and even though she didn't answer, she surely has the messages by now. This is the first time I've driven down to the college by myself, but the GPS lady will get me there easily. Today they could go out to eat and do some shopping and I will hear all about college and then tomorrow we will go to church. Surely Jasmine has a church picked out by now.

She had not asked Jasmine where she was going to church, knowing that she wanted to ask, but she had wanted to respect her daughter's privacy, but this weekend, she would find out. They would go to church together and she, Joanne, would feel better. Joanne pulled into the dorm parking lot, turned off the lady in the box, and got out of the car.

~

Jasmine picked up her phone and listened to the message. "Jasmine, I'll be there mid or late morning. Looking forward to catching up. See you soon." Her mother did not ask if she was busy, but just announced she was coming. Jasmine lay in her dorm room bed, listening to the quiet. Her roommate had gone home for the weekend, and the quiet soothed her and frightened her, both at the same time. Her mother had left two other messages, but Jasmine had not answered the phone, wanting instead to listen to the quiet, listen for the still small voice, and decide what she should do this day. These few weeks she had been in school, she had spent her weekends trying to get to know the town, the school, and trying different activities.

She knew many of the kids, reveling in their freedom, were into experimenting with things she wasn't experimenting with. But she was interested in the campus hiking group, and they were going to the top of Pike's Peak. But, her mother was coming.

I wish she wasn't coming. All my life, my mother has been calmly and cheerfully guiding my life, knowing what was best for me. There isn't much danger in me doing some of the stuff other kids are into — I'm not going to turn to alcohol, sex, or drugs, but I'm just interested in figuring out my days, especially my weekends. Hour by hour. With no one choosing my schedule but myself.

Someone knocked at the door. Just the knock felt like an intrusion.

"Jasmine, are you in there?"

It was Cassidy. "Come on in."

The door opened and a chubby smiling girl walked in and looked around. "What are you doing, lying there on a Saturday morning? Chop-chop! Let's get moving. Some of us are going to a free concert downtown in the park. We're going to take lunches and pretend to study. I thought you were going?"

"Yea, I was, but my mother's coming. I wish she wasn't, but she is on the way."

"Did she ask? Did she give you any warning?"

"No, and not much."

"Well. Okay. I'll see you later." She smiled her sparkling smile, and left.

Jasmine turned over and waited.

~

Joanne knocked on her daughter's dorm room door, and waited, and then knocked again. When the door opened, Jasmine was on the phone. She smiled at her mother and motioned her in.

"Yes, yes, I can do that," she said into the phone.

Joanne walked over to the window and waited, careful to not look around too much. The room seemed fairly neat, but she didn't like the posters on the walls around the roommate's bed. Current rock music confused her, and the posters were a part of that. Dark -- they were dark, and Joanne wondered why teenagers couldn't be more cheerful.

Why couldn't they like cheerful music? Had Jasmine gained a bit of weight?

After Jasmine got off the phone, she invited her mother to sit down.

"Here's the box of things I thought you might like. I especially thought you might want the wrist brace," said Joanne.

Jasmine nodded but did not look in the box. "How long will you be here?" she asked her mother.

"All day. I thought I would spend the night, and go to church, too, and breakfast." Jasmine didn't show any emotion. *Surely Jasmine wanted to do these things with her*

"I'm pretty busy this weekend, Mom. Why don't we go to lunch right now and have a good talk. I'll bet you're tired. You had to get going early this morning to be here at this hour. There really is a lot to see and do in this city that you might find interesting, but Mother, I have plans for this evening and tomorrow morning. But you can have fun without me."

"Let's go to lunch," Joanne said abruptly.

"Sure," said Jasmine as she stood up, grabbed her backpack, and then opened the door for her mother.

Joanne stopped at the door and said, "You wouldn't believe how hard I've worked on that house. And can you believe it? After all these years, someone dared to move in next door and plant trees along our property line. You wouldn't believe all the leaves I've cleaned up."

Joanne then marched down the hallway with Jasmine following her. Joanne continued her narrative about the house, all the way to the car.

"Where are we headed?" asked Joanne after she settled behind the steering wheel.

"How about a steak house I heard about?" asked Jasmine.

"That's fine." Joanne started up the car and at the same time continued her monolog about the house. She carried on while Jasmine fed her the directions, and did not stop until they entered the parking lot of Bill's Steaks and Sandwiches.

Once inside, a waitress directed them to a booth situated next to the window, and handed both women menus as they nestled into the booth's seats. Joanne studied the menu, afraid to say anything, knowing she was walking in new territory and not knowing what the territory actually was.

Jasmine said, "I need some energy, which I guess is my way of rationalizing that I am about to order a big breakfast."

Joanne squirmed in her chair, knowing she was stalling for time and her dignity. After they ate, Jasmine would have no more use for her. Her daughter was going on with her afternoon, and Joanne had no idea what she was going to do.

"Well, it pains me, but I'm ordering oatmeal." Jasmine had obviously gained weight and needed her mother's good example. How could she have gained weight when she was walking everywhere? Joanne let her words, her good example, lie there, without belaboring the point as she often had done in the past, but Jasmine didn't seem to notice or show any inclination to change her order.

While they waited for their food, Joanne talked more about the house and the neighborhood.

"Mom, I really appreciate your coming down this weekend. I know it has been a tough time for you, and I'm glad to see you are surviving. I need to get back to the campus soon, however. I've got several commitments."

So, her daughter was not going to change her mind? After all she, Joanne, had done to make this trip. Joanne searched for words. Jasmine didn't even offer what the commitments were. *It would be nice to know more details about my daughter's new life, but she's hardly said a word.*

"Of course, I'm disappointed. We haven't seen each other in a few weeks, and a lot in our world has changed."

They continued to eat. Joanne could see the pained expression on her daughter's face.

"These things affect you, Jasmine. I have your best interests at heart."

"No, you don't, Mom. Not really."

Joanne, stunned, put down her fork. "How could you say that?"

"It's like you walk and talk with a Christian mirror surrounding you. You are so conscious of teaching, helping, and being a good example, that you can't see me. It's always your agenda."

"I don't know what you're talking about!" Sounding gracious seemed impossible. Joanne could feel the blood in her veins freeze.

"I know, Mom. And that's what's so sad. Look, even when we ordered, you did it with an attitude of teaching me and maybe you didn't say anything overtly, but it was all about influencing me."

"I don't think so. And even if it's true, why not? I'm your mother. Knowing what's best for my child is my duty."

"Why not? It's like you invade my space without even trying. There's no place for me and my mind to just be."

"Jasmine, I'm not here to have an argument. Neither one of us needs that. But the fact remains. We have had a lot of changes, there are going to be more. Your father is pressuring me to sell the house, and we must talk about these things."

"No, Mom. You may need to talk about these things, maybe with a professional, maybe Dad, but not with me."

"Excuse me? You're saying I need to talk to a professional? I can't believe you said that?"

"Look, Mom, I don't mean to insult you, but I just think you really have been through a lot, and if I'm letting you down, then I think you still need to talk to someone. You shouldn't have to do life without someone to talk to."

"What are you saying? I think it is so important to keep you informed. When I was growing up, we didn't talk about anything. Anything meaning important issues, and some, I might add, looked small but they weren't."

"I think, you really believe that, Mom. And I really believe you had a difficult relationship with Dad. I get that it has been hard on you, but you brought your hurts and pains to me, because you didn't have someone to talk to. In some ways you married me. And I bought into it. But no more. I got it a long time ago that your marriage was not so good, but I no longer want to be your earpiece, the one who tries to help you feel better."

Joanne continued to eat. She would not let her daughter see her get upset. But what was her daughter saying?

"Let's lighten up the conversation, shall we?" said Joanne brightly.

"Sure. Which of my classes would you like to hear about?" asked Jasmine.

"Why don't you just start at the beginning of your week, like Monday?"

Joanne didn't hear her daughter as she talked. Joanne's mind roamed in a frightened manner, knowing something was terribly wrong. Was this her daughter? She had heard of kids changing when they went away to college. Is this what they were talking about? She kept waiting to hear Jasmine make her feel better, but it didn't happen.

When Jasmine took a break from talking, Joanne started in, as cheerfully as she could, talking about her early days in college. She talked of her roommates, the clothes, and how dating was different. She talked and they ate, and the time passed.

"I've probably goofed, talking so much about myself. You know, of course, that your best interests are of the utmost importance to me. That's always the way I've been. Have you picked out a church, yet?"

"Mom, I know you're trying to be helpful."

"Kids can get in a lot of trouble in college."

"I know, Mom. I know you are scared to death I'm going to get involved with drugs or sex without you to guide me. But I need to think my own thoughts, now."

The conversation stumbled after that — Joanne paid the bill and drove them back to the dorm. She clumsily hugged her daughter, said something positive, and then she left as fast and gracefully as she could. Terrified that she had now lost everything dear to her, she drove carefully through the city and entered the highway, but then the tears started and wouldn't stop. She pulled over at a rest stop and let the tears flow. The grief of so much dying at once, finally filled her heart to overflowing, and the tears went on and on.

The phone rang. She could hardly see to find it, through the tears. It was her cousin Andy.

"Where are you? I'm leaving in the morning. Class ended a few days early. We need to say goodbye. Are you spending the night there? Are you crying?"

"I had planned to stay the night, but I'm coming home. I'll be home in a couple of hours. Is your invitation still open?"

"What invitation?"

This was not a good sign. "Surely you remember inviting me to Crystal?"

"Sorry. This class has been hard on my brain. Of course, I want you to come to Crystal. I need the help and it'll do you some good."

"I don't know about that, but I need to leave. I know that."

"What happened? Did your visit with Jasmine not go well? I hope she doesn't already have a boyfriend. That's almost always a disaster when kids first leave home."

"No, it isn't that. I actually don't know what it is. I'm so surprised. I already have lost so much, and I had looked forward to spending time with her. We needed to reconnect — but it was obvious I had intruded on her time. She actually said some horrible things to me. No question I was glad to get out of there. I wish the problem had been as simple as a boyfriend. She said I needed to talk to a counselor."

"Come on back to the house," said Andy. "Don't drive until you've stopped crying. Don't rush. I'll help you get packed up and deal with the house, Larry, and everything you need to tend to so that you can leave with a good conscience. We will leave the next day, and we'll have a good time."

"How can that be? I'm a mess. And I don't think we can get everything done tomorrow."

"Nonsense. It's just a house. It's just stuff. And you're entitled. It's been a long haul, and time for a vacation, if you can call it that. Mainly it's time for a change, and listening to God."

"I hate everything Jasmine said to me today. I don't need any more of that. I don't hate my daughter, of course, but I need to go far away from here, far away from my daughter and Larry. Are you sure you are fun on a road trip?"

"I have been told I'm a veritable blast on road trips. One man entertainment, with wisdom beyond my years, and we can call my new kids on the phone when we get bored. They're pretty funny."

"My ex-husband will be mad at me."

"Well, call him tomorrow and get the whole thing worked out. It's my understanding you have fulfilled all legal obligations for now, so if that's true, and he still stews about something, well, it's on him."

"Easier said than done. I hate to hear him stew."

"Careful here, cousin. I may agree with your daughter."

"About what?"

"That you need a counselor. Get a grip, call him on the phone tomorrow, and tell him where you are going to be, and give him my phone number. Cell service doesn't work in Crystal. You'll be back home in a few weeks, the house will sell fast, and you deserve this time off, or, if he would prefer, you can get a good start on a nervous breakdown, start an expensive counseling session, and send the bills to him."

"You mean I could leave and not fret about anything? I'm under no obligation to get the house in shape and sell it immediately. I know that, but I can feel his disapproval." Joanne dabbed at her eyes, feeling the tears coming again.

"I do like that word fret. Good use of it in Psalm 37, I believe. Don't fret about anything, but let God stay up all night worrying about it. Or something like that."

He waited until she spoke. "I would like to go. I'll take enough clothes for a couple of weeks. I won't have a car, though."

"You won't need a car. It's a small town. I'll make sure you get a ride to the airport when you need to return to Denver. I'm happy about this. Don't rush. I'll see you later tonight."

Joanne sat on the side of the road a long time, until she had no more tears left. They fled slowly, and when her sobs finally subsided, she felt totally drained. She couldn't move. All she could do was be aware of her own breath. She was breathing. Her phone rang again. Jasmine this time. Joanne did not answer it.

She checked herself in the mirror. She looked awful. Her phone rang with a third caller. Larry. She took the call.

"Joanne, what the heck is going on? Jasmine called, upset about your visit, I couldn't make out what she was saying or what she wanted me to do. What's going on?"

"What's going on is I am closing down the house for a few weeks, and when I get back, I'll get it ready for a glorious open house."

"You can't be serious. We agreed -- "

"No, we didn't Larry. I didn't agree. I was silent, but I didn't agree. But I am telling you now, I need a few weeks away, to adjust to everything that has happened. When I return, I'll get this house sold for top dollar. You will be happy with that. Until then, you can reach me through my cousin Andy in Washington State. Goodbye, Larry."

Joanne looked again at herself in the mirror. Who was that sad person? When did she get so much older? She turned the key, started the car, and entered the freeway. She didn't need the GPS lady to tell her the way home.

∽

Back at the house in north Denver, Andy contemplated the refrigerator. He would help the process along by eating food that might spoil, and then cleaning out the thing, except for what they needed to pack for the trip tomorrow. *Thank you, God, for your timing. Thank you for working on the daughter -- may Jasmine grow, in her new environment, into the person you want her to be. I pray for this family, Lord. In the meantime, thank you for providing the help that I need. And thank you for this class, that is now, thankfully over. Thank you for my cousin, the new house church, and the safe journey for my cousin and myself. She's wearing to be around, Lord. Please help me to be patient.*

CHAPTER 4

ON THE ROAD TO CRYSTAL, WASHINGTON

"You doing okay?" asked Andy.

"Sure." That was a lie. Joanne knew she wouldn't turn back. But she was scared to be starting something new. Andy drove through the mountains like an expert — that wasn't the problem. To be going out of state and leaving everything important to her behind in Colorado was so frightening — that was the problem. Staying home, that would have been way too painful — she knew that, but taking off, like this — it felt like she was falling off a cliff.

She closed her eyes as Andy drove over and around the Rocky Mountains, and reminded herself why she was doing this thing. She couldn't deal with it all anymore. The house, worrying about what people think, her daughter, and what to do with her hair, which was so very gray. *When did that happen?* All of the above were twisting her up. The somewhat funny thing about it all was she obsessed about her hair and the trauma of whether to color it or not. She had always had shiny brown hair, carefully turned down on her neck in a tasteful bob, and now it was gray, and the gray had a strength to it, almost like wire. The wiry hairs had a mind of their own and didn't lie down smoothly.

When did her hair change so much? Why did everything have to change? And all at the same time?

"I'm proud of you," said Andy.

"I can't imagine why," said Joanne.

"Because here you are. I was hoping, as difficult as yesterday was, that you would keep on keeping on, and tie up the loose ends and be on the road with me today. If you were tempted to change your mind, you didn't let it show."

"I was tempted. Yesterday, even more than my court date, was the true shutting down of so much. And to do it in one day. And, to get packed in the same day for a whole new location and life-style. Do you know how long I would spend getting ready for one of Larry's and my vacations?"

"Let me guess. Three or four days?'

"Try three weeks, of planning, getting things to be altered, shopping, having our guest bedroom full of suitcases, clothes laid out, and lists on the wall. And that was just for me. I had Larry's to do, too."

Andy didn't seem to need a map or the GPS lady, plus he didn't need to talk. By the time they were driving west through Wyoming, the incessant chatter in Joanne's head actually slowed. The fast-driving Andy took them down the highway and Joanne slowly started to relax and notice the relentless stark landscape.

"I've never noticed so much land, asphalt, and trucks before," she said.

"Are you hungry?" he asked.

She thought about that. Was she? She always ate by food groups and knew what she should eat at certain times of the day, but being hungry? She didn't know. "What time is it?"

"I'm not sure," said Andy. He laughed. He didn't question her. He seemed lost in his own thoughts. They traveled on until they saw a sign, "Big John's Truck Stop Four Miles Ahead."

They pulled in, circled the large flat building, found no parking, and so Andy drove into the back lot, filled with trucks lined up, their diesels running.

"I've never stopped at a truck stop before," said Joanne as she took in the massive amount of trucks in the parking lot.

"I don't want to park way back here," Andy said. "Let's try again." He drove again to the restaurant and found an empty space next to the building.

Joanne got out of the car, stretched, and then walked with Andy to the door. A large man with a beard and a big smile burst through the door and held it open for them. Andy thanked the man, took Joanne by the hand and they walked inside.

As the waitress led them to their table, Joanne absorbed the environment, so different from her usual dining experiences.

"I really never thought of women being truckers before," she said as she looked around the large room of people eating and talking. "And look at that! A sign pointing to the showers. Makes sense. I just never thought of it."

After scooting into their booth, and looking at the menu, Joanne decided to not say anything about the food to Andy -- that wouldn't do, but she sighed deeply as she looked at the selection offered -- heavy, heavy, heavy salad dressings. Large servings. Fried food. Friendly people, though.

On the second day they were driving through the mountains of Utah, still green with only a smattering of snow on the peaks.

Andy didn't talk much, and Joanne got tired of hearing herself talk, so she watched the scenery go by. She had never taken a long road trip like this. Traveling was done through airplanes and taxis to and from the airport. It was hard to absorb how much land there was, and people living off the land.

Andy's phone rang as they drove down the mountains to Salt Lake City. He put it on speaker.

"Hello," he answered.

"Heh, Andy, this is the two kids that love you most," said a girl's voice and a boy's, speaking in unison.

"What are you two up to? Getting your homework done? Helping your mother?"

"My life sucks," said the boy.

"My, my, what's going on?" asked Andy.

"My history teacher gave me a C on my research paper. I don't think it's fair."

"So, what was the problem?"

"I've been sick and didn't have enough time to— "

"Hold that thought for a minute," Andy said as he swung into the left lane to pass a truck. Then, after returning to the right lane, he said to his new son, "Okay, go ahead."

Then the kid went on for a long time with his litany of problems. Andy asked a few questions and occasionally he said, "That's terrible." He smiled at Joanne every time he did this, as if they held some secret between them.

Finally, they ended the call.

"I thought he would never stop. He's got quite a load," said Joanne.

"He's a good kid. You watch. He'll likely call back. Maybe by tomorrow. He'll have some good thoughts. He just needed some empathy."

Joanne didn't think so. She would have told the kid what to do, what to say to his teacher, and that would have been that.

Ellen and Sally drove to the back of the motel and parked in front of cabin 11. They unloaded without any chatter between them, and then once inside, talked over the agenda for the next few days.

Sally, knowing her next assignment shouldn't be put off one more day, loaded up her art supplies and drove to the most important neighborhood of Crystal — their adventure could not begin any other place. There she set up her easel on the side of the road, pointing toward the ancient house in front of her, with the picturesque barn in the background, and the mountains beyond that.

She hadn't been painting long, when she saw the little girl and her mother, walking between the houses toward her.

When they got closer, Sally said, "Hello! I just love the view from here. Do you think anyone minds my painting here?"

The little girl and her mother approached. Bingo. Sally knew them from their pictures. Rebecca, the mother, introduced herself, and her daughter, Clarin.

"No one minds you painting here," said Rebecca. "It's a compliment, actually. That's our house, in back of you, but that's our barn and pastures in front of you. You can see them between the houses. The original farmer sold off some lots and then his house burned down. Some day we'll build a house next to the barn."

"It's so lovely, and makes a nice walk for you. Absolutely charming. Would your daughter like to try painting?" asked Sally.

"Can I, Mommy?" asked Clarin as she imploringly looked up at her mother.

"That looks like expensive watercolor paper, to me," said Rebecca.

"It will help me out. I need to get started and I'm having a hard time." Sally smiled at them both. "Here's what you can do, to help me get started." Sally filled her big brush with water and then in beautiful glowing blue paint and then she scrumbled the brush messily across the paper, creating a blue joyful blob.

"Wow," said Clarin.

"Now, you do it, over mine, or anywhere you want," said Sally.

Clarin bit her lip thoughtfully, and then took the brush from Sally, swirled it into the water, pushed it around in the paint, and then giggled as the brush transformed the paper.

The Great Salt Lake looked different from the highway instead of the view from flying over it, as did the high desert of Oregon. From the highway, Joanne was also aware of the people. Many people, living in towns, driving the highway, on their way to work, to run errands, just as she would in Denver. Maybe they had sick parents to take care of, or sprained ankles, or dinner to cook. Joanne was amazed at the people busily moving about and doing things.

Andy entertained her with tales of his previous road trips, including his honeymoon, which was to Canada, and at his wife's request they stopped at every local museum in every community, no matter how small.

"What was she doing? How tedious was that for you?" asked Joanne.

"She was actually working on a history paper for her master's degree," said Andy. "She looked specifically for relics from the first settlers of the community, specifically china cups and saucers. She was interested in the tough journey the women had made and how much of their previous culture they had brought with them. Especially the delicate little cups and saucers."

"Oh," said Joanne. She had never thought about that.

"Did you find a lot?"

"Not a lot, no, but frequently there would be one or two in a case. Quite a touching testimony to how the frontiers of Canada and the United States were developed, and the cost to the women."

Indeed. Andy did not seem irritated with her, even though her questions would likely seem disrespectful of his wife.

Through Oregon's high desert, she saw cowboy country, and that surprised her. Cowboys were part of Colorado, or New Mexico, California, Arizona, Texas, and other states, but she had never thought of Oregon being cowboy country.

Before they stopped driving for dinner and the night, Andy's son called back. Joanne was driving this time and Andy didn't put the phone on speaker. She could just hear his side of the conversation, which included numerous "uhuhs" and several "Sounds good to me."

After he ended the call, she asked him, "How did that go?"

"Pretty good. I tried to listen to him. He had some new good ideas since his previous call, when he was feeling so sorry for himself."

"Weren't you tempted to tell him what to do? He's got college in front of him, if that's what he wants, and teacher issues can be important."

"Sure, he's looking at college in a couple of years. He wants to be a vet. But if he's going to trust himself and God, without me or his mother telling him what to do, he has to begin now, and it's my job to help him in that process."

"That's what I did with Jasmine," said Joanne.

Andy did not reply. They stopped for the night, ate their dinner and then went to their separate rooms. The next day she would see the Columbia River and from there the big forests of western Washington and then Crystal. Tomorrow would be a big day. She was amazed at how silent her phone was. No phone calls about anything from anybody. Her daughter, her ex-husband, the church, the neighbors were all doing fine without her. The only call had been Andy's son. That unsettled her. Where were all the people who cared? What if a giant truck hit them and that was it? Would anybody care? Would there even be a short tasteful service at her church?

She went to bed with more questions than answers. And she was frightened. She had thought she had understood Andy, and that they had Christianity in common, but she didn't get what he was about now. She doubted his way of dealing with his son, and she wondered about his effectiveness as a pastor. That alone unsettled her, but that added to the new community she was about to join, the new people, and she slept fitfully. Andy, his being different from what she thought he was about, that was the most disturbing thing. He was supposed to be her rock during this time, but he wasn't. Her ex-husband had always had the answers, the plans, and now she leaned on Andy, and he wasn't measuring up.

Andy got up excited. He was getting tired of his beloved cousin, as much as he loved her. One more day of driving and they would get to Crystal and then the next day he would drive on by himself to Port Tiffany and see his wife and kids.

When they got down into the breath-taking Columbia Gorge Joanne admired the huge river and the gorge, but then she started talking again.

"There wasn't anything I wouldn't do for Jasmine or my ex-husband. I can remember how heart-breaking it was to get the news from the doctor that I couldn't have any more children. It broke my heart because I knew my husband wanted another child, and I knew that she wanted, desperately wanted, a brother or a sister."

"But what did you want?" asked Andy.

"I wanted to create this beautiful family, and I was devastated that I had let them down."

"Was that, in your mind, a turning point in your life?"

"Of course, it was! How could you even ask?"

"There are different ways to look at things."

"Oh, no. There are not, for some situations in life. They are black and white. And this was one of them. Believe me. I know what I'm talking about."

Andy just listened. She was in no mood to hear a different opinion. He had seen it many times.

They continued their journey down the gorge, admiring the huge river and the massive path it had carved over many thousands of years. They talked about the history of the area, including Lewis and Clark, and Andy was grateful for the change of topic. He could hardly wait to see his beautiful wife and kids. He had been away too long. They hadn't been married very long, but they fit into each others lives easily and joyfully. What a lucky man he was.

"You're thinking about your wife, aren't you?" asked Joanne.

"Yes, how did you know?"

"That smile. Hold on, pastor. We'll get you there. I'm just glad you found someone that makes you happy."

"She's amazing. I hope we have many years together. The kid thing is good, too. Two very nice teenage kids. I'm sorry for their earlier sorrow in life, losing their dad. But I am awfully lucky."

∼

HOME OF THE BEARS

Totally awesome. Totally unreal. Standing on top of Mount Kendrick beat any other experience in Jasmine's life. She could see the tops of the mountains all around her, and out onto the plains. The view and the thin air added to her giddiness.

"Is this your first Thirteener"? asked Mrs. Hull, the staff sponsor of the hiking club.

"It is!"

Mrs. Hull was short and stout. She had churned her way up the mountain easier than some of the kids, moving like a jeep.

"Be careful going back down, that's even harder. And be careful of the after-hike party. That can get a bit out of hand."

Jasmine resented that. Did she look totally incapable of being able to handle herself? She could handle herself. She didn't need another mother.

"Hi," said a male voice. Jasmine, who had been carefully watching where she put her feet on the way down, looked up to see a tall, thin red-haired boy. He smiled at her and she smiled back, uncertain what to say.

She stayed with the group, although she didn't have much to talk about, and the red-haired boy stayed quietly by her side. When they reached the parking lot where they had parked their cars, the talk turned to where they would have pizza and beer. Jasmine felt good in the group. They shared a common interest in the environment and the physical challenge.

"My name is Jeff," said the red-haired boy. "Would you like to ride down to the pizza place with me?"

"Sure," said Jasmine. She had ridden up with one of the adult sponsors, and didn't want to do that again. She would not, however, let it be too friendly. A couple of the other boys were very cute, very talkative and funny. Her interest lay with them.

One of the girls that Jasmine was getting to know said quietly to Jasmine as they rested before finishing the descent, "Some of these guys are really cute and they especially got my hormones going when I first got here. I had to learn that as strong as that was, it was still just a distraction from why I was here."

I resent that. I like it that this cute red-haired guy is interested in me. I like the way he looks at me. He doesn't talk much, but he's always watching out for me. I can handle boys. Jeff is not as exciting as some of the others, but he'll do for now.

∽

Andy drove north, leaving the Columbia Gorge and moving into the great forests of Washington. The freshness of the air, and the knowledge that they were getting closer to Crystal revived both of them.

"Would you like to know something about the people you'll meet?" asked Andy. "There's a lot of special people there. One of them is Tyler. I told you a little about him the other day. He's the young man who is missing part of his left arm; he has a prosthesis." His passenger did not respond, but seemed only interested in looking out the window.

Andy kept driving, enjoying that his passenger was so excited about her surroundings. They drove into the mountains, winding higher and higher, hemmed in by the dense forest. When they started back down, Andy found a wide spot and pulled over, so that Joanne could see the picturesque valley, and nestled deep in that valley lay their destination, the little village of Crystal.

"It's beautiful," Joanne said. "It's dreamy it's so beautiful. Nothing in Switzerland is any prettier than this."

"Lord, thank you for our safe travels. Thank you for the opportunities that lie ahead. We thank you for helping us serve you. Thank you for Jesus, Amen." After Andy finished praying, Joanne joined in.

"Lord, thank you for this new opportunity. May I always carry your name and glorify you. I want to help build this church. I want this community to be better for my being here. Thank you, Jesus."

Andy again silently thanked the Lord for their safe journey, and asked for continued blessings. They then began the descent, winding down through the deep forests, across an ancient bridge and on through the forest and valley toward the village of Crystal. The leaves were turning on the maple trees and smoke curled from the farmhouse chimneys.

They had talked a lot on their trip from Colorado, and she shared as honestly as she could about her life, the disappointments, but she had no insights on where she hoped to go. She had talked of her faith, and disappointments, and she did talk a lot. *I am more and more weary of her, but she is the closest thing I have to a sister, and I love her. Help me Lord, to be patient with her limited self-righteous thinking. I know you've been plenty patient with me in that area over the years.*

But what concerned him was how sure she was that she was right about everything. While he didn't condone anything her ex-husband had done, he knew that she was also difficult to live with -- she was so perfect, so quick to sense another person's needs, to follow through, she didn't leave any space for other people to be themselves, to live with the questions in life. She preached salvation to the extent other people felt like she was smashing it down their throats. And then she did her best to live in that person's space, guiding and softly manipulating.

No doubt Jasmine felt the same oppressiveness. Joanne's disappointment with her visit to her daughter's college was painful to listen to, but Andy made no inroads on her attitude. Joanne easily moved from knowing all the answers to being a victim, and there was no in-between.

Andy knew he could not make her way in Crystal. Joanne would enter the town, and either learn something or not. Either way, she would be a help to him, and hopefully, *hopefully*, she would benefit from being away from Colorado for a few weeks. She was stubborn, not self-reflective, and he hated to admit it, but he needed a break from her. And he had prayed more times than he could count, *Lord, help me, help me deal with my beloved cousin. She is wearing.*

They drove through the outskirts of the town and Joanne remarked, "I'm glad to be out of the thick forests. For the most part, you can't even walk in these forests; they are so thick with trees and whatever. In Colorado, at least you can see into the forest and probably walk into it.

You couldn't walk into this if you wanted to. And even if you did, you wouldn't be able to see a bear if it was six feet in front of you," she said.

"Paths are very important in this forest, for that very reason. Crystal is surrounded by forests so deep that you can't really move in them. Don't get lost."

"I'm frightened. It's been a long time since I did anything on my own. But I will be helpful to you. I promise you, Andy, I won't let you down."

Andy could tell she was frightened, but not of these people, this small town. It was frightening for her to be out of her world, a world of Colorado, Jasmine, and her ex-husband where she knew the dance that she did with each one. But this town and these people, she would have new things to learn. If she was open, she could handle it, and God would show her the way back to Colorado. She could have a better life. Andy knew she wanted to be proven right, to be vindicated here in Crystal. Her self-worth, her self-esteem, needed that. Or so she thought. Andy knew differently, and Andy knew unless she could learn to hear the still small voice of God, she would not learn what God wanted her to learn. Andy also knew that he was in control of none of it. It was totally out of his hands. He could see it, but he couldn't bring it to pass, and he wondered what God had planned. He did not wonder long, however. He was tired, ready for food and sleep, and ready to see his wife and kids the next day. Whatever unfolded in Crystal and how his cousin dealt with it, would not hinge on him at all, and he was grateful. Playing God wasn't his idea of a good time.

"What's to eat in this town?" asked Joanne while she stared at all the quaint buildings.

"The best chicken pot pie you've ever tasted," said Andy. "And I could eat three myself. Next stop, chicken pot pie."

After they settled into their booth, the waitress approached.

"Pastor Andy! You're back! Did you miss me?" the waitress asked with a big smile. She was about forty years older than Andy and moved with the speed of a turtle.

"Of course I did, Agnes, and if I weren't a happily married man, I would be even happier to see you."

Agnes rolled her eyes and looked at Joanne. "Who is this?"

"This is my cousin. She's going to be in the house for a few weeks. Treat her nice, Agnes. I like her."

∼

After they ate, they drove to the center of town, marked by a stoplight. "This is the only light in town," he said. "The schools are down that way; the grocery store and the hardware store are down that way." He pointed the other direction. "But we go this way." He drove east, past little stores, and back into another neighborhood.

"There's a church!" she said. "I thought you said there wasn't a church in Crystal?"

"That's now the town museum. This town's history is full of logging, hunting, and now, people who want a hiking adventure."

He turned off the main street, drove four blocks and stopped in front of the house, a glorious if run-down house, with a stone fence, and large porch, and two stories. Maybe even a third story? The two big maple trees in the front yard frosted the grass with red leaves. She looked, without saying anything, or getting out of the car.

Finally, she said, "We're here. And I have the funniest feeling that I am about to have the biggest adventure of my life in this little town. So very odd."

Andy, aware that God could be planning such an adventure for Joanne, once again said nothing. He knew what odd plans could be on God's list, but there was no way to prepare for it.

Andy got out, went around the car, and opened the door for Joanne. She stared up at him. "You're very patient with me. Don't think I haven't noticed."

He put out his hand and said, "Cousin, get up, get out, and come see your newest project."

She sighed deeply, took his hand and got out of the car, and then shut the door.

"You're stalling," he said.

She took his hand again, and walking hand-in-hand, they made their way up the sidewalk to the front steps. She paused and then mounted the steps with him.

As they stood in front of the door, Joanne said, "From one house to another." Andy saw the tears in her eyes, but said nothing. He unlocked the door and held it open for her. She took a deep breath and stepped inside.

~

Inside the front door, she found herself in an old-fashioned entryway, old-fashioned in that there was no open concept. A crystal chandelier hung from the tall ceiling. To the left she opened a door to see a large living room with a fireplace, a faded rug and overstuffed furniture — enough chairs and sofas to seat twenty people. Built-in bookshelves lined the walls with many, many books. Joanne approached them and saw titles from *History of Egypt* to *The Power of Positive Thinking*. She would explore this later.

"What do you call this room?" she asked Andy.

"The library is fitting, don't you think?"

She nodded and they continued back to the other side of the entryway where double doors opened to a large room, a large dining room. No table, no chairs, but it would take a big table and many chairs. This was a room with possibilities.

She turned to Andy, who quietly followed her. "This is fantastic. Utterly fantastic. The entryway, the grand library, this dining room. Not modern, not open concept, but how perfectly wonderful for a house church. I'm so excited." She did not wait for him to respond, but moved around the room, looking out the windows. "What pretty views, what a grand place for everything from potlucks to bridal receptions. Oh, my! And I can find a table, I know I can!"

Back to the entryway, she passed the staircase and a powder room and entered a huge room that went from one end of the house to the other. A huge room, with another fireplace, meant for large gatherings. She could see why Andy thought this would be a good church house. She almost floated around the room, looking out the windows, picturing the people, and the joy that would develop in this room. She could picture Andy sharing his messages here. What kind of seating? No matter, that would come. What was with these old carpets? To be figured out later.

Joanne went into the kitchen, once again not open concept, but a large room all on its own. Long, running along the side of the house, with lots of counter space, wide windows against the wall, old-fashioned tile on the counter tops, and a small table with chairs. Joanne opened the pocket door at the other end of the kitchen, and there was the dining room. Perfect. She closed the door and opened the smaller pocket door above the counter there, and once again saw the dining room. Even more perfect, a pass through. So lovely, so practical.

"It takes my breath away, it's so wonderful," Joanne said to Andy.

"Let's go upstairs, and then we'll get the suitcases. I'm about to crash, but I am happy that you are so excited about this project."

Upstairs she found a landing that surrounded the staircase and off of that were four doors — four bedrooms.

"Each bedroom has its own bathroom," said Andy.

She wandered into each one, quite similar with heavy old drapes, hardwood floors with faded rugs, and furniture that needed serious evaluation. So much to look at and think about. So much wonderfulness and potential.

"I made sure the bones of the house were good before we accepted it. In other words, things like electrical, plumbing, termites, etc. have all been evaluated and taken care of."

Joanne nodded, but hardly heard him. She went back to the bedroom that was over the dining room below.

"Can this be my bedroom while I'm here?" asked Joanne as she looked at the small bedroom and the faded blue drapes, bedspread, and blue roses rug.

"Sure. Good choice. You can look out these windows and keep track of the town."

They stood side by side, looking out the window.

"I'll do well here. I'll work on the house. I can see your vision. The bones of it are wonderful."

"Just to have it cleaned up a bit, evaluated, will be a big help. I don't even know if there's a coffee pot in the kitchen. I need to turn in, and will likely leave in the morning for Port Tiffany before you get up, but I thank you for your hospitality in Colorado. And, if you think the house is amazing, wait until you have time to explore the backyard. It's a mess, but there's a greenhouse back there, and besides the garage, there is a small apartment that used to be for servants."

"My ex is going to be having a fit," said Joanne.

Andy sighed. "I know. But you are on solid ground. Remember that. At this point, it's more about you than him. While you think you are here to help me, consider this time as helping you."

She didn't say anything. Andy knew she wouldn't. She was in God's hands. He wanted to see his wife, his kids, and he knew he couldn't fix Joanne. Time to go to bed. He took Joanne's hands in his and said, "Dear Lord, thank you for our trip. Thank you for my cousin Joanne, and may you bless her and keep her as she works in this house, all to your glory."

And Joanne added, "And Lord, may you also keep Andy safe as he travels back to his wife and kids. And may everything I do here be to your glory and bring more people to you."

They brought their suitcases upstairs and retired to their separate bedrooms. Andy left her in God's hands. God's very capable hands. God knew what was needed in Joanne's life and he did not. He slid into sleep easily, thinking about his wife, their kids, and how close he was to their home.

∼

Joanne got up before daylight, found the instant coffee in her suitcase, and a teakettle in the kitchen.

"Wow, you are efficient," said Andy as he stared at her from the door.

"There's a travel cup right there, for you to take on your way. Sorry, no food yet. But I do think there are some books from the library you might want to take with you." He nodded and left in the direction of the library.

Joanne continued to putter in the kitchen until Andy reappeared.

"Where did you get the boxes?" Andy asked her.

"In the hall closet."

Joanne helped Andy load his suitcases and three boxes of books into his car.

They stood facing each other. "I'll be back for Thanksgiving with the family, and we'll have a big dinner. I hope you are here for that."

"I don't know about that. But it will be ready for you. This house will be the place of many souls being saved for Jesus."

He reached out and hugged her, and said, "Try thinking this way, Joanne, think of the house as a place where people learn to see each other, love each other, and serve each other."

"Of course. That's what I just said." She planted a kiss on his check, and he drove away.

Joanne watched him drive away and felt a sense of abandonment. She had a task, no car, and knew no one in this town. The sun was just beginning to lighten the sky, a new day, a new beginning. *Where should I start?* Probably the little grocery store wasn't even open. Well, she could do without food for a while. She set about sweeping the porch that ran on three sides of the house. When the sun got higher, she would get some food. For now, the porch would be swept, and then she would attack the house later. It was too glorious to go inside.

Joanne continued sweeping, moving rocking chairs, empty planters, and watching the sun come up. The cool sunny day reminded her of Colorado.

A little girl, maybe four, and her mother came up the walk.

"Hi! I'm Rebecca and this is my daughter Clarin. You must be Pastor Andy's cousin."

"Come on up," said Joanne, "and enjoy the newly swept porch."

"And we brought you fresh-baked cookies and a thermos of coffee."

"Fantastic! Instant only works for so long."

Joanne brought three chairs together, and took an empty pot off a small table, which she then placed in front of the chairs.

Joanne was immediately taken with the little girl, who so politely sat down and then passed the cookies, while her mother poured coffee for herself and Joanne.

"My daddy has horses," said Clarin.

"Really? Do you like the horses? Are they big horses?" asked Joanne.

Clarin looked very solemn. "The horses are very big and I don't like them very much."

"I have a daughter, much older than you are. When she was little I tried to get her interested in learning to ride horses, but she didn't care for it. I even bought her a pony, a very well-behaved small pony, but she would have none of it."

Joanne happily took the freshly baked cookies they offered her. They chatted about the history of the house. The old couple who lived there had no children in the area, but the children had grown up in Crystal, and had donated the house in remembrance of their parents.

"We came to meet you and welcome you, and invite you to the music recital on Sunday afternoon, this coming Sunday. Clarin is playing the piano," said Rebecca.

Joanne smiled at Clarin. "Wow, you play the piano? How old are you, Clarin?"

Clarin smiled, showing her dimples. She held up her hand with four fingers.

"There will be other students. Five, I think. Clarin has only been playing for a few months," said her mother.

"I will be there. I can't think of a better way to spend a Sunday afternoon. Would you like to see one of my first projects for the house?" asked Joanne.

The cheerful group went into the house, and Joanne opened the doors into the dining room.

"Oh, wow," said Rebecca. "This is huge. No wonder Andy wanted this house. This is fantastic. I can already hear the happy voices that will eat here."

"I know. It's sort of old-fashioned and wonderful at the same time, isn't it? Look at this, Clarin." On the dining side, the pass through looked like a picture, a picture in a frame of a pretty scene of lambs playing in a field. But when Joanne pushed it open Clarin clapped her hands with glee. She pulled the one chair in the room over and climbed up on it and leaned on the sideboard. "Look, Mama! I can see the kitchen!"

Rebecca shook her head and smiled. "Unbelievable and perfect for what Andy wants. You could even have a small wedding here."

"Will you be coming here, for church I mean?" asked Joanne.

Rebecca said, "Well, not for church so much. Tyler's a bit reluctant on that. But, we're friends with Andy. So, you know, we'll be here. I wonder if we might not have a slab of wood in the barn that would make a good table top. Tyler and his helper, Deet, work with wood, making custom cabinets, and they mill their own lumber. Would you be interested in that?"

"That would be wonderful, I'm sure. I've got to get to work on the whole house, but within a few days, I'll be seriously interested in a dining table. Andy wants to have a big dinner here on Thanksgiving."

"Tyler's out of town with clients in the mountains. Why don't you come by when you have a chance, and we'll see if we can work out a table?"

Joanne watched them leave, holding hands, and talking happily about the recital, and Clarin's new dress. What nice people in this town, thought Joanne. *I'm going to get along here. I will be useful here.*

After Joanne watched them head up the sidewalk, she sat down on the porch and finished the cookies and drank the coffee they had brought her. Joanne then retreated to the kitchen to clean and get it evaluated. The cupboards, were bare, no crumbs, no signs of bugs or mice. The stove, an ancient old gas stove, sparkled. The refrigerator, an ancient chipped thing, hummed along and looked clean, but Joanne knew she could never be peaceful unless she had disinfected all surfaces herself. She found cleaning supplies under the sink, and proceeded to do just that, even the inside of the stove and refrigerator. She then swept and mopped the floor. With that satisfaction, she decided to do a quick cleaning of the bathrooms before she went into town for food. The four bathrooms and the powder room were old and dated, but were all scrubbed. But still, Joanne quickly disinfected everything. And then she knew she was past due on real food.

There was something charming about the hardwood floors and the area rugs. Obviously wool, some plain and some floral, the rugs must be worth a fortune. Lucky she was here — she would do a good job for Andy. Not just everyone would know the value of those rugs. So happy to be taking charge of this house, she almost forgot her next task, which was to walk into town.

Joanne put on a light jacket and walked into town, enjoying the town, the fresh air, and saying hello to the people she passed. At the grocery store, she started to get in line, but gave way to two other women also needing to check out.

"I'm in no hurry," said Joanne.

"Neither are we. We're in town for a few weeks."

"So am I! My name is Joanne."

"I'm Sally, and this is Ellen. We're here just to paint for a few days."

"Oh, I can see that. It's beautiful here. I have no talent, but I appreciate art."

"We're landscape painters, except I like more abstract landscapes," said Sally.

Joanne saw the clerk patiently waiting and stepped up with her groceries. As she walked back to the house with her two bags of groceries, she thought about the two nice women she had just met. Even the visitors here were nice. She thought about the painting lessons she had taken over the years, and wondered about taking it up again. She already loved this town, the house, and the nice people she had met. At first, she had been scared to death of the whole thing, and afraid of not having cell service for her phone, but now it seemed like a great thing. If her ex or her daughter wanted to get a hold of her, they could call Andy and he would get the message to her through any number of people in town.

But for now, she was safe, and not having to answer a phone was a plus, not a liability. Surely, she deserved that after all she had been through, after all she had lost. The peacefulness here, the nice people — this was just what she needed. God was very smart.

Back in the house, she put the food away, heated up a frozen dinner in the microwave, and ate her lunch on the porch, waving at the neighbors and introducing herself when they ventured over. She liked the quietness more than she thought she would. No TV, no radio, but she could hear birds. After she cleaned up, she went into the library/living room. *I would love a fire, but that will have to wait until the chimney is inspected.* She looked at the books on the shelves and wondered about the people who had lived here, and then she settled into a chair with a book about the history of the tribes in the area. Soon Joanne fell asleep.

When she awoke, the sun barely peeked above the mountains. *I've been very tired and slept for a long time.* Without getting up from her nest, she glanced around the room. Who were those people who had lived here, and what kind of paintings did they take with them, the faded walls showed there had been paintings there, or maybe it was photographs? Family photographs? And why did they leave all these books? These books needed to be evaluated, and that would take time. No doubt some would be very valuable, as would the two large chandeliers. And what about this rug, this huge floral, faded, rug? Joanne slipped down to the floor and felt it. Wool. Yes, valuable, and later she would search for a tag or a name on it. Right now, however, her job was to dust. She would dust the books, the shelves, the chandeliers. And after that, she took all the chair and sofa cushions outside and pounded them. She dusted the baseboards and crown molding, and then she vacuumed. She moved every piece of furniture and vacuumed, being ever careful of the wool rug that was so large it almost covered all the wooden floor.

She decided to eat some of the salad she bought from the grocery store, and then suddenly she was enveloped in what felt like a whole year of tiredness. She quit for the day, picked up her book, and wearily climbed the stairs to her bedroom. *God, give me wisdom, wisdom in how to get the house ready for people. Give me wisdom in dealing with all these people in this new town. Thank you, God, for this chance to serve you. I am falling in love with this town and the people already.*

Joanne got into the bed and pulled up the feather comforter. She opened the book but, unable to focus, she put it down. *I'll shut my eyes to rest for a few minutes.*

∼

Tyler saddled a horse while Deet watched, his arms across his chest and his hat low over his face.

"Why exactly are you watching? What good are you?" asked Tyler.

"I'm watching you to see if you do it right. I'm the deputy sheriff in this county, and one of my jobs is to make sure you saddle horses correctly," said Deet.

Tyler laughed. "Tell me again. Why you wanted to work with horses, be in the forest, and help me. Why didn't you stay with boats?"

"It was your friend, Collin. I learned from him to reevaluate my life. When I did that, I knew that for my final years, I wanted to return to horses. I started my life with horses and I'll finish with horses. I prefer horses to boats."

"And this is because you think horses are easier to get along with?"

"That is an incorrect analogy. I may not be an educated man, but I like my analogies correct. Here is the correct way of saying it: Horses are easier to get along with than with the *Pacific Ocean*. That's correct English."

Tyler started on the next horse, brushing him down swiftly and carefully. His prosthesis didn't hinder the manner in which he lovingly and expertly took care of the horse. "Yeah, Deet. Tell me why you won't ride back with the women. Tell me that part. I've forgotten."

"I like women just fine, but they can get strange around horses. Like it seems to me they need to find their lipstick at the most inopportune times, forgetting the needs of their horses. I don't have any patience with that."

"Are you guys talking about me?"

Tyler and Deet looked up to see Mary Dixon, one of their clients. A second-grade schoolteacher, Mary had a no-nonsense, but fun attitude.

"I can assure you that I have found my lipstick and will now saddle my own horse." She smiled brightly, proceeding to brush her horse.

"I guess I've just been shown up," said Deet, as he saddled a horse. Deet and Tyler finished with the last horse together. They then started packing the camping equipment and putting it in Deet's truck. They had just loaded up the last of the equipment when the other two campers, two women, arrived laughing between themselves.

"Did you ladies get the pictures you wanted?" asked Tyler.

"Yes, the sunrise was phenomenal on the river. We didn't see any animals, though,"

"As a county sheriff, as your helper, I wish all of you a safe trip back. I don't apologize for taking the easy way back, and I'm glad to see that you all have had a good time. May it continue." Deet tipped his hat, got in the truck, and took off with his load.

"He's quite a character," said Mary as she watched Deet drive off.

"Yes, he is," said Tyler. "But as old as he is, he is really valuable in this county as a deputy sheriff. And he's very helpful to me."

"Do you wish you had a younger man sometimes?"

"Not often. He knows a lot more about these mountains, and horses, and people than any younger man would. And he has no interest in the women. I don't want any of the flirting or problems a younger man could cause."

She nodded and mounted her horse. "I want to thank you for doing this. I may not do anything like it again in my lifetime."

Deet continued down the mountain road with his load of camping supplies. He liked Tyler. He even loved him. Not only because of the admirable way that Tyler functioned with one complete arm, although that was impressive. Tyler saddled a horse, shot a gun, put up a tent, Tyler did everything without making a big deal out of his arm. In fact, it was easy to forget there was a hook where a hand ought to be.

Tyler didn't talk much, loved his wife and daughter, and always moved with integrity. Deet was glad to be off the island, working with Tyler, and also play at being a deputy sheriff.

I'm an excellent sheriff with a truck and nothing much to do.

Deet drove back to Crystal, happy to see the gate and know that he was home. He drove in and saw Clarin playing with the chickens in the barnyard. He knew Rebecca would be close by, and found her sitting in the shade of the barn with another woman. Who was she? He parked the truck and gave Clarin a pat on the head.

"Tyler and the women are doing fine," he said to Rebecca. "They're on schedule."

Rebecca introduced Joanne and mentioned how they had been looking for a large table top for Andy's house.

"That's awfully dirty and heavy work in there, trying to just see all the wood Tyler and I have available. Let's go in now and I'll show you some hidden stuff."

Behind the barn was the workshop, and Deet was actually proud of how clean they kept it, the wood stacked neatly by type and sizes. He pulled out a wide plank. "This is maple from a ranch near here. It's beautiful wood and rare, being maple and from such a big tree. We have enough planks here to make a long wide trestle table. What do you think?"

"That would make a gorgeous table. What would it cost?" asked Joanne.

"I'll talk to Tyler about it. He's pretty fond of Andy. I wouldn't worry about it."

He watched Joanne and Rebecca talk about it, and then they left with Clarin. He didn't quite like the new woman, Joanne, although he couldn't exactly say why. He liked Andy well enough, but he wasn't sure about Andy's cousin.

He unloaded the camping equipment and stored it in the barn. He would repack it later, but for now, his part of providing the ultimate western experience was over, and Tyler had the hard part. The women would live out of what they could catch in the river and the supplies they had on their horses. The luxury part was over, and he was glad. When they returned in a few days, the season was over for Tyler and Deet. Other guides in town might take out hunters, but not Deet and Tyler.

He fed the horses and then decided to get a quick nap. It had been a long, hard camping season, and he and Tyler were ready for the winter. They were ready to work indoors and make cabinets. Or tables for pastors. He was getting older, too, and not as patient as he used to be.

He watched Joanne and Rebecca walk with Clarin back toward the house. Rebecca was one fine woman, and she sure made friends fast. Maybe too fast.

~

Joanne and Rebecca talked while Clarin skipped along in front of them, stopping frequently to pick up pretty rocks.

"Look, Mama! It's Sally!" Sally was indeed painting near where they had found her painting before. She waved at them.

"Do you two know each other?" asked Rebecca.

"We met at the store. We are fellow travelers and newcomers," said Joanne.

Joanne and Rebecca walked over to where Sally had set up her things and admired the painting, although it wasn't finished.

"Would you both like to come eat with Clarin and me?" asked Rebecca. *Why am I saying this? Because I like them, and I want their companionship, that's why.*

"I would, but I would also like to not have you working," said Joanne. "I can go to the restaurant and bring something back."

"I agree," said Sally. "It would be fun to eat together, but you don't need to work on our account."

Clarin pulled at her mother's sleeve. "Mama, can I show them my train?"

Rebecca felt so tired she couldn't imagine actually fixing dinner for someone else, but she liked the thought of older, caring women and their companionship. And Clarin? These women added to Clarin's life.

"I won't cook. You are right. I'm pretty tired, but I do have some leftover lasagna in the fridge. Warming it up won't be hard. Would you mind making the salad?"

"I'll be right along," said Sally. "Let me call my mother. Sounds like a perfect meal. And I do know how to make a wonderful salad."

"Did you want to ask Ellen to come too?" asked Rebecca.

"No, she has plans. I'll be right there. And I want to see that train set."

Joanne, Clarin, and Rebecca walked slowly on, enjoying female companionship and the ease of the evening. When they got back to the house, Rebecca curled up on the couch and enjoyed easy conversation between Joanne and Clarin. By the time Sally arrived, Rebecca was half asleep, and a peaceful sense of well-being and being cared for enveloped her. *I'll wake up when I smell the lasagna heated up.* She drifted off to sleep.

When Rebecca slowly came to, a few minutes later, it was indeed, the lasagna's fragrance wafting through the house. She slowly sat up and looked around. Ellen and Clarin were placing a vase of flowers on the table, and Joanne stood by the table serving the salad into bowls.

Lovely.

CHAPTER 5

Clarin, on the day of her recital, grew tired of waiting for her mother and decided to play with the cat. She threw the red ball, and the large fluffy white-haired cat chased it, and almost caught it, but Clarin pulled the string attached to the ball and the cat followed, chasing, pouncing, all the way back to Clarin. The cat lost interest and rubbed up against Clarin, purring and happy to be with the little girl, who sat on the floor, waiting for her mother to take her to the music recital. She petted the cat until he decided to lay comfortably on her skirt, and that is where they were, looking like a picture in a magazine, tiny little girl, hair in curls going down her back, her blue dress spread around her, the cat on her skirt, the cat's white hair all over the blue velvet dress, when Rebecca came in.

"Are you ready to go, pumpkin? You look so pretty and I know you're going to play pretty."

Rebecca looked at herself in the mirror, adjusting her hair and earrings.

"I wish Daddy could be here," said Clarin.

"I know. He wishes he could be here. Well, let's go." With one last look at herself, she then looked down at her precious daughter, who now stood beside her, looking up at her mother with solemn eyes, and

Rebecca could see the beautiful blue dress was covered with white hair. Long white *cat* hair.

The horror Rebecca felt, the tension of it, was just about to erupt out of her mouth and it was just by the grace of God, she didn't say what she was thinking. *Clarin, how could you? This recital is important, and I took such pains to find this dress for you, fix your hair, get you ready for this event, and you couldn't stay away from the cat for just a few minutes. Clarin, what the hell is the matter with you?*

Only God could create the miracle that came out of her mouth.

"Clarin, sweetness, I need to run the roller over your dress. Wait here. I'll be right back."

When Rebecca promptly returned with the roller, Clarin asked, "Are we going to be late?"

"No. Not at all. We only have a few blocks to walk." The sticky roller ball was full of white hair and most was off of Clarin's dress. *Good enough.*

They put their coats on and set off, Rebecca holding her daughter's hand, both silent until a handful of leaves rustled across the sidewalk in front of them.

"Mama, can I kick the leaves?"

"No, sweetness, not today. Let's not scuff your shoes up today."

"Can I tomorrow?"

"Yes, you can. Tomorrow will be fine."

"What time will Daddy be home?"

"Your bedtime, I think."

"In time to read me a story?"

"I doubt it. But I promise, even if you are asleep, he'll come in and kiss you goodnight."

"Does Daddy miss us when he's out working?"

"Yes, he does. Lots."

"Would he rather think about his work or me?" asked Clarin.

"Look at it this way. When he's working, he needs to think about working, so that he can do a good job, keep people safe, and that's what we all need to do –- focus on the moment at hand."

"Like when I'm playing the piano?"

"Pretty much. That's right. When you're playing the piano, you need to focus on that and not think about Daddy, right?"

Clarin kept walking; her head down. She mumbled something.

"What did you say" asked Rebecca.

"I said I miss Daddy, I like the way his shirts smell, and I'll think about him tonight until he comes home."

Rebecca smiled and said, "That sounds good to me. Let's focus on this evening, but when it's all over we'll think about Daddy."

Joanne wore her best sneakers and her black pants and sweater. Important to not dress up too much in this community, but she was excited to be going to this recital. The school in Crystal was for elementary and middle school children, the high school kids riding the bus down to Landing. Joanne walked into the town center and then walked past it for three blocks to the older brick two-story building, with a new wing that housed the school cafeteria/gym, which served as the setting for the recital. *This is the meat and potatoes of life. This was not show; these people didn't even know the meaning of the term. These dear people were here, surviving, and looking to support one of their own. I am here. I am a part of it. I can help.*

Joanne entered the room with excitement and trepidation. This many people, the whole scenario made her nervous, but as soon as she entered, the friendliness of the crowd warmed her heart. The piano teacher approached her first, and then she had to keep moving, even while people stopped her to talk, people telling her *I've seen you walking, are you Andy's cousin? I'm so glad we are going to have a church in town.* She finally got to a chair, almost feeling like she was a rock star, the friendly welcoming way the people of Crystal treated her.

Then she saw Clarin and Rebecca, sitting in the front row with the other students and their parents. Joanne couldn't imagine a cuter little girl. How did it happen, other than a gift of God, that Clarin could play so well at four? It would be interesting to see how the evening went, with several beloved children playing, but Clarin being the obvious star. Jealousy could be ugly and devastating.

The first three kids played the piano. Joanne joined in the applause after each one, and said a silent prayer for each family. She did the same for the next two kids who played the violin. Respectable performances by all, but it was clear none of the kids were really excited about what they were doing. The discipline, the knowledge of music, the poise developed; all was important and always needed to be acknowledged by the audience. The teacher introduced Clarin, and Joanne sat forward with excitement.

Then Clarin walked up to the piano, and everything changed. Word had spread, and the room became totally quiet and focused. Clarin looked like a tiny doll at the piano. She smiled at the audience and then turned to the keyboard, and "The Flight of the Bumble Bee" took off and floated through the room. Clarin focused on the piano, the music soared, and joy filled the room, in a way that Joanne was only used to experiencing in a concert hall with professional musicians. It was mesmerizing and hard to not be happy for her parents, Rebecca and Tyler, and sorry for the other kids and their parents. *I hope they won't be scarred for life*, thought Joanne. She forgot the trauma in her own life and listened to the little girl play with remarkable joy and skill. Music, good music, warmed Joanne and settled her down, even when it was music played by a tiny little girl.

When the little hands stopped, it took a few seconds for the magic to stop ricocheting around the room. And then the applause started. Joanne had a tough time not standing up, whistling, and stomping her feet. But the applause stopped at an appropriate time and all the other kids came on stage for their final bow, and the applause picked up again.

As the applause ended, Joanne thought of punch and the refreshments table, but she couldn't move from her chair because of the people who wanted to say hello. Those who didn't welcome her when she came in took the opportunity to welcome her now, slowing her progress to the punch bowl. They offered help if she needed anything. Some she had met before, and some were new. She talked to each of the kids who had played and their parents, saying something gracious to each. What a happy friendly community event. *Now, time for the punchbowl.*

"Very good teacher, don't you think?" asked Ellen, who had already discovered the cookie tray.

"I think so, in more ways than one. She brings out the most in each one. Of course, Clarin being the star, she has to be careful."

"Yes," said Ellen. "That little girl obviously has a talent and the teacher obviously has a challenge, to nurture her but also be attentive to the other kids. But when Clarin plays, it's a whole other deal. Of course, all of the adults have the same challenge, to not fuss over Clarin too much." Sally and a couple Joanne didn't know, joined them. "Yes," said the man, "I only hope her parents can get her the training she needs as she grows. You would not want her to lose that."

Ellen beamed. "She's quite remarkable, isn't she?"

"She's more than remarkable, and she needs the best lessons possible," said another woman. "I know that Tyler and Rebecca struggle, but this lesson thing is important."

One of the other fathers joined them, and the topic of conversation quickly changed. When the proud father moved on, the group returned to discussing Clarin. The group grew, and the consensus was that Clarin needed the very best lessons, and that was that. This was something Joanne knew a lot about. She could help here. *It will be subtle, but I will help make sure this little girl has the best musical training. I know how to talk with people, talk with Rebecca.*

Joanne put on her jacket, talked briefly with Rebecca, and said her goodbyes again to the music teacher. She stood at the door, reluctant to leave. She had purpose here, and Andy had known it. Dear, sweet, wise, and wonderful Andy. Pastor Andy. *My cousin, who loves me.* She surveyed the crowd, and then left the building. The happy crowd had spilled out onto the patio, and the night air glittered with stars and laughter. As she walked home, she thought about her work at the house, the dear house, and how it had all taken on a new meaning as she had gotten to know the people. And maybe, just maybe, Andy would see his way to having some community events in the new church house. That large room could be large enough for events such as recitals, and be more intimate. She could see a piano at one end, the fire burning, and in the dining area, food for a reception. It was perfect. Of course, these would have to be things Andy would decide. And his wife, of course. She didn't know much about his wife, but this was a modern age, and pastor's wives didn't have to be an extension of their husbands anymore, playing the piano and teaching Sunday school. Maybe Andy's wife wouldn't care. Maybe she could just focus on influencing Andy. Joanne had never felt this joyful and this safe. This town had done this for her. Andy's effort to get her here was so well-founded, and she didn't think that much about her ex-husband or her daughter as she walked along.

The main thing was clearly this -- that she get onboard for supporting the talented little girl. Ellen was right, that was a priority. To be a part of a young child's life was the utmost of trust from the Lord Almighty and Joanne needed to prioritize that. Some of these people, dear people, weren't as educated and traveled as she was, and she could help this effort to make sure that Clarin got the support she needed. She knew nothing of Tyler, but he had not made it home for his daughter's recital, and that left him lacking in her eyes. *And I know how to make things happen. I know how to get things done in a church or a community.*

In the dark of the fall night, Joanne stood under the streetlight, looking up at the house. It looked magical, the stars surrounded it, and the graceful old face lit up by the streetlight. The leaves on the ground rustled gently in the breeze. Someone had lit a fire, and it smelled wonderful. Joanne continued up the sidewalk, up the steps, and turned to look at the town, sparkling with the ordinary lights and the hopes of the coming holidays. *All this is new to me, people are gracious and I am a part of it. I like the thought more and more of making the house "church."*

Joanne went inside, and draped her jacket over the bannister. It was time for chamomile tea. *I really must get that fireplace checked out and some firewood in.*

Tyler loved his beautiful wife and daughter, and Clarin was his daughter, no question about it. There was no other father. He had married Rebecca before Clarin was born and he never asked her who the biological father was. If Rebecca wanted to keep it to herself, that was her business. He loved her, they married, and the three of them were a family.

He was around women all spring summer and fall, taking them on horseback rides into the mountains, and he worked hard to give them an experience they would cherish for a lifetime. He wanted to foster their appreciation of their horses, the beautiful Olympic Peninsula, and the fellowship of whatever group they were traveling with. But he was never, ever tempted. Not that certain things weren't offered, but he always handled such things with firmness. Tyler believed in honor and integrity, and that was the only way he wanted to live.

But now, he was home, and he was ready for the peace and quiet of winter and ready to work with Deet on his custom cabinet business. He was good with woods, and enjoyed the work. The wood he used was local -- he milled it himself, designed and built the cabinets himself with the help of Deet.

He had just stepped off the step, headed to his barn, when he heard the phone ring. He hesitated briefly, heard Rebecca answer, and kept walking until he heard Rebecca call his name. He turned around.

"It's the governor's office," she said. Her face unreadable.

"The governor of Washington. An aide. He wants to talk to you," she said.

What could this be about? Tyler returned to the house and took the phone from his wife. "Hello?"

"Tyler, this is Mitch Brady at the governor's office. The governor has seen a table you made at a friend's house, Rich Stevens."

"Oh, sure." Rich Stevens, owner of the largest computer company in the world. He couldn't forget that. "That was a fine piece of wood that Rich brought in. My pleasure to work on it. What can I do for you?"

"The governor liked it very much, and would like a similar table in the governor's mansion. It would be a wonderful addition to the mansion, and a tribute to the craftsmanship of Washington State, and our beautiful forests."

"What exactly are you talking about, Mr. Brady?"

"What I'm suggesting is this. We don't have a lot of money to put into art. The state needs to spend lots of money on other things."

"I understand that."

"But, here's what we offer. If you could procure the wood for the table, one way or another, we would pay you for your work. I'm sure your work is going to be worth a lot more, but we also offer this. Free advertising. Your name in full view in the mansion, a press release on the whole deal, and tv coverage when it is installed."

"This is sounding good to me. What are the dimensions you need for this table?"

Tyler wrote down the information and took a deep breath. After he told Rebecca what was going on, they both looked at each other with wide and shocked eyes.

"This could really turn into the best advertising we could ever have," said Tyler. "And it would go on forever."

"Do you have the wood for the table already?"

"I don't know. I don't think so. I'll go to the barn right now and see."

As he left his house to walk to the barns and check on Deet and the horses, Tyler felt great. He was home and he could do what he wanted. And he had before him the chance of a lifetime. He walked a couple of blocks to where Deet lived. The barns, the pasture all belonged to Tyler, and Deet lived above the main barn. Deet took care of the horses and the barns and the chickens and also did his part time work as deputy sheriff. All that, along with helping Tyler with the furniture/cabinet making business and helping with the camping business.

He saw, before he could go in and check his horses, the three women he had taken on the campout, and felt somewhat dismayed. He had thought they would be gone by now, but there they were, one horse loaded into their horse trailer, and the second one was obviously not interested in loading into the trailer, or anything else probably. The third horse stood quietly, his eyes half closed, bored by the scenario.

Tyler arrived and watched them. He then approached the woman trying to get the horse into the trailer, and asked if he could help her. She handed the lead to Tyler and backed off. Tyler sat down on the edge of the trailer, gave the horse room to relax, and found a piece of licorice candy in his shirt pocket. While the horse relaxed, Tyler focused on the candy, stuffing the wrapper in his pocket afterward. After a while, Tyler got up, stretched, and sauntered over to where the horse stood, eyeing Tyler. Tyler talked softly to the horse, rubbed the horses neck, and then behind the animal's ears. Tyler said something to the horse, tightened up the lead and started up the ramp. The horse followed him. He then calmly led the horse into the trailer and tied the lead.

He proceeded to the other horse, but that horse also balked at going up the ramp. Tyler sat down on the ramp again, let the lead go slack, and calmly talked to the horse. After a while, he got up and repeated what he had done before, and with all three horses in and tied, Tyler shut the gate.

"I get what you just did," said the woman who had most joined in the work on the trip. "You don't need to say anything. I got it." The other two women waved and got in the truck.

"Hope you come back next summer," he said.

"If I don't, please remember what I experienced and learned will last for the rest of my life," she replied. She got in the driver's seat.

He watched them turn in the driveway as he held the gate open for them and as they drove past him, he said goodbye and waved. Now it was time to talk with Deet about this new table and how it was going to change all their lives.

Tyler found Deet cleaning a horse's hooves.

"Deet, we have to talk. I think we have the chance of a lifetime."

Deet took his time straightening up. "The older I get, the more I could use 'a chance of a life time.' I take it you are talking money."

"Not that we won't work, but it will be easier than what you're doing right now. Finish up there and meet me in the woodshop."

Tyler was going through the wood in the shelves when Deet showed up. "We've got some good wood here."

"Wait!" said Deet. "Before you start committing that wood for whatever your new project is, we have a prior commitment."

"Like what?"

"Andy's new house. The one they will turn into a house church. He needs a long trestle table for the dining room. Something that will seat a lot of people or provide buffet space."

"Who said this? I thought Andy wasn't showing up until Thanksgiving."

"Right. But he has his cousin there for a few weeks, and she's evaluating the house and getting it cleaned up for him before they open the church, and she said she needed a table for the house. That's when I said he's a favorite of ours, and I thought we could provide a table."

Tyler thought about that only briefly. "I'm not interested in any church, but I sure agree we can provide that table. Andy may not get me into church, but otherwise he'll have my loyalty."

They pulled out the long boards, choice boards that they had cut down, hewn themselves, and stored to dry a year ago. It would be a huge table, seating twenty people. They then discussed how they would make it. The very best for Pastor Andy.

"All right, that's been decided. And we need to have it ready for Thanksgiving dinner. What's next? What's this great opportunity that will make your life and mine easier?" asked Deet.

"The governor's office called. For display, for use, they want us to build a table out of old growth cedar for the governor's mansion. Our name's will be on it, we'll be paid for our work, the advertising effort will be wonderful, but we have to provide the wood."

"First of all, tell me why and how our names came up for this honor?"

"Remember the computer guy that bought one of our tables? He socializes with the governor's wife or someone close to the governor. They have a program -- they have been looking for local artists, and somehow our names came up."

"That seems odd to me."

"I know it. It's not as if we have won any contests or anything. But having high-end clients works, and word travels. There's no way this can't be a good thing."

Deet made a low whistle. "Wow. Let's figure this out. Do we have the wood for that table?"

"Well, no. Out of our very fine stash, we do not."

"I know who does. Gordon Greeber!"

"That guy. What does he want for it?"

"I'll find out."

"Do that. And don't let him know what it's for or the price will go up. Why don't you go right now?"

Tyler stepped outside and opened the gate for Deet. He shut the gate and started walking home when he saw a woman he didn't know walking toward him. He was used to being approached by women who looked like this — expensive jeans and expensive haircuts.

The woman extended her hand and then introduced herself as Andy's cousin, Joanne.

"I'm glad to meet Andy's cousin," Tyler said. "Andy and I go way back and I would do most anything for him. Which is why I've already started on the table."

"I'm loving this town," said Joanne. "The people, the house I am working on, and I'm so glad to meet Clarin's father. What a talented daughter you have!"

"I know. She's quite the girl in many ways."

Joanne proceeded to tell him about Clarin's recital and how wonderful it was. He knew Clarin had an exceptional gift, and he hated not being there to see her. The way Joanne kept stressing Clarin's need for a teacher bothered him, though. It was like she knew best what his daughter needed — he had no patience for it. He ended the conversation and returned to his barn and looked at the message board. Nothing from Deet. The horses were happy in the pasture. He went into his workshop and inspected the maple cabinets that were almost finished. This was his art. This was what he looked forward to finishing this winter. This would pay for anything Clarin needed. This was his love. He didn't love the horses anywhere close to what people thought he did. He loved them all right, but they were mainly tools, and when he had to put one down, like he did a couple of weeks ago, it wasn't as traumatic as people thought it would be for him.

He checked phone messages, checked the fire alarms, checked the feed status, and then returned to look at the horses one more time. The horses looked wonderful. They watched him, waiting to see if he signaled them to do something, or maybe he had a treat. They saw nothing and returned to grazing. He decided to write one note on the board to Deet. *Buy more batteries for the smoke alarms.* Everyone knew why he was constantly taking care of those smoke alarms. He would be that way all his life. You lose your dad and part of your arm to a barn fire, and that's just the way you are.

CHAPTER 6

Tyler sank down into the lounge chair, leaned back, and put his hat over his face. This was his front porch and he didn't care if he moved the rest of the afternoon. Good things were drifting out of the house; fragrances only Rebecca knew how to create in the kitchen.

"Daddy?" A voice quite close to his ear startled him.

Tyler lifted his hat and saw the big eyes of his daughter, only inches from his.

"What, darling?" She was so beautiful, so wonderful, so interested in the world.

"Mama says she and I need to go to the store for your favorite something. I forgot what. We'll be right back." She smiled uncertainly.

"I'll bet you delivered that message just right, baby. I'll just wait right here until you get back."

She gave him a kiss, and ran back into the house. He waved at them as they drove away in the car. He tried to read the paper, but the desire to take a nap overtook him. Is this what happens when you get older, he asked himself, or is it just that much work to take a group of women camping? He had just relaxed into a deep sleep when he heard a car drive up. The car parked in the driveway and an older woman Tyler didn't know got out. He stood and went to meet her.

"I'm Ellen," she said as she held out her hand. "My daughter-in-law and I are in the area to do some painting."

"Sure. I remember my wife saying something about meeting you in town. What can I do for you?"

"I've heard about a special northerly trail, seldom used. I wonder if you could get my daughter-in-law and me up there. I'd like to check it out for a possible painting retreat next spring."

"We could get snow any moment. You're attempting a lot this late in the season."

"I know. I imagine you'd like to forget it until spring."

"Let me get this straight. You are asking for the ride up to the camp we have. And then walk the north and very difficult trail from there. There would be no camping. We would have to hike out to the coast, which is very rough, get down to the beach, and hike into the next town, which is Landing, probably in the dark. And you want to do this because why?"

"The ruggedness of it appeals to us. It should be a unique place for a unique painting retreat. We have to plan now, we have to advertise soon."

"I'm not all that interested, Ellen. The season has been long."

"I will pay well, very well. Your daughter is going to need the best quality music lessons and this will take care of that."

This was the second woman who took an interest in telling him how to take care of his responsibilities and he didn't like it. He didn't need any woman telling him what he needed to do for his daughter. "I'll think about it and let you know." The conversation was over.

She hesitated and then left. Tyler returned to a chair on the porch, put his feet up on the railing, closed his eyes and tried to sleep.

He had just nodded off when another vehicle approached, and this time he knew who it was. Deet.

Deet got out of his rattling truck and walked up to Tyler.

"Watching your legs carry you around is like watching an eggbeater try to walk. Did you get that bow-legged from riding horses or from trying to stay upright on boats?" asked Tyler.

"I was born this way. Convenient for entertaining people. I just checked on that wood you're interested in. The price is pricey." When Deet told him the price, Tyler shook his head. "That's pretty high. Not that I blame him." Tyler looked out at the sky figuring the numbers in his mind. "I'll have to think about it. In the meantime, that brown mare has thrown a shoe. Do you want to try one of those new shoes?"

"Yeah. But I'll have to put on two," Deet said. "Did I see that artist woman leaving here?"

"That's right. She wants to take a quick look at the north trail. Wants to take a look at it before the snow falls."

"You're kidding me?"

"No, and she wants to do it in one day."

"Well that's a heck of a day. Why is it so important?"

"Look, I can't speak for people and the way they want to spend their money."

"We were both ready for a rest from all that. Speaking of money, what's she talking about?"

"Plenty. Would provide a lot for my women. Especially those music lessons Clarin will need. Everyone in town seems to think they need to voice their opinion about that to me. And of course, there's the wood for the table for the governor. It would solve a lot of problems. Fast."

Deet turned and started back to his truck. "I'll get started on the mare and her shoes. You'll make a good decision. Don't let anyone push you around. If you decide to do it, take extra insurance. You and I may work hard for every buck we make, but we do all right. Don't let anyone else's panic push you around. You know where to find me."

That's what I like about Deet. He trusts me. He doesn't try to push me around, even though I'm younger. I've been lucky to have good men around me, and that includes Deet.

CHAPTER 7

Dennis watched the three men, one on the dock handed the grocery items to another man on the boat, and called out the name for the third one to check off his list. Dennis had thought this out carefully, and the food had to be right. He wasn't doing this second best.

"What's this applesauce?" Dennis asked as the applesauce was handed to the man on board.

"Look, I didn't pick it out. It was what was already in the truck."

"Nice," said Dennis, "but that doesn't fly with me. It says here on my list, unsweetened applesauce, and this is clearly, clearly, sweetened with extra sugar and cinnamon added. This is not what I ordered and you need to take it back."

The three men glowered at him.

"No, wait. We'll go through the rest of the order and make sure there aren't any other mistakes."

After setting aside the applesauce, they went through the entire order, finding hot dogs with nitrites, which Dennis had specifically said no way to, and bread with far too many additives.

"I'll take the rest of the order below, but you need to take these back and get what I ordered," said Dennis.

Do the right thing, that was his motto, and he had hours to spare. He didn't even know what plan was in place yet. Now it was his turn to wait for the phone call.

He took each box of food down into the galley, and then put each item away. He checked the cooler. Plenty of meat and it was getting ripe. Enough to feed a bear and then some.

When the men returned with the proper food, he gave each one a tip and then after they climbed back to the dock, the last one turned and yelled up to him, "You're kind of familiar looking, don't I know you from somewhere?"

Dennis shook his head. "No, I'm nobody." The other man walked away and Dennis went to the wheelhouse and started the engine. He checked -- all of his equipment was ready to go, time to set off for Landing. From the deck of the boat he loosened the lines gracefully, without having to get off the boat. He then backed the boat up, slowly, so as not to attract any attention. Out of the marina he went, patiently stopping and waiting on two other boats. *My life is just about to get extravagantly wonderful, and I have all the patience in the world for you who are ignorant about boating etiquette.*

Out beyond the breakwater, the sea roughened. The sun peeked through the clouds, and seagulls swarmed overhead. *You think I have something to eat, but you're wrong.* He steered the boat north, and she bounced steadily along, on his way to Landing, his destiny, and a new life.

After three hours of the choppy water and listening to the diesel engine, Dennis was starting to feel a bit queasy.

He got a brief phone call from Sally; she needed the boat's name and their arrival time.

The rough water, and feeling sick wouldn't stop him. There was nothing to do, but take another pill and keep going. He was trying to deal with that and keep the boat on course, when Sally called back. She said she needed the name of the boat again. *I love her so much, but when she gets nervous and unfocused like that, especially today, I could lose my patience. Who knows who might have been listening to our conversation on the radio?* He flatly told her again and then the radio went silent.

Dennis entered the small bay, and thankfully the waters smoothed, somewhat, but not much. *I've never docked a boat in such rough waters, and I have to do this right. I can't cause a problem or bring attention to myself or the boat by ramming someone's boat. Headlines here or anywhere, "Rock Star Can't Park His Boat" would be a disaster.* He lowered the throttle, and approached an empty space. A man stood nearby, watching a sailboat as it approached. He looked at Dennis's boat, but didn't move. Dennis knew he was on his own. He eased forward and was within seconds before he remembered the fenders. He turned the boat back out to sea, got all six fenders down, three for each side, just in case he needed to change sides, and then he returned, easing up to the rocking wooden platform. Dennis jumped off the side, stumbled, and then tied down one line and then the other. The man who had been waiting to help get the sailboat securely tied up was now locked into an argument with the captain of that boat. Even though the sailboat was now successfully tied up, their heated argument kept them occupied and neither one noticed Dennis. "I am blessed with the purpose of this adventure," said Dennis to himself. *All is going well.* He climbed back onboard.

Inside the boat, he got out the large backpack, the one with the frame, and loaded the meat into the pack. His personal items had been packed weeks ago. Now it was plenty heavy but he was capable of carrying it all. He got the heavy pack up to the deck and then went back down below and checked everything. All was perfect. Everything was ready. Even the little white stuffed lamb. He put it on the pillow of the small bunk and smiled. Yes, he was ready.

Out on deck, Dennis climbed down the steps and then reached for the large backpack. He put it on and took off down the dock to find the office. When he found it, he filled out the form, put the money for the moorage in the envelope, and put them both through the slit in the office door. The dock master, still busy with the sailboat, waved at him, but continued helping with the sailboat and its inexperienced crew. *Good, less attention toward me.* Dennis continued until he came to the steps that would take him down to the beach. The waves hit the shore with power, but there was plenty of space on the beach for walking, and he set off, down the beach on the gray day. He wasn't the only one, and no one paid him any attention. One couple walked their dog; another man looked down at the sand as he walked, either looking for something or watching his steps carefully. Dennis watched them, but they didn't seem to notice him. He kept walking and soon left Landing behind. Down the lonely beach he walked. The heavy backpack was not too much for him. Those months of training were worthwhile. He was blessed. Amazing how well everything was going, and he knew that was a sign, a sign that everything was blessed, and worth it. The stars were aligned in his favor. He didn't know a lot of religious talk, but felt comfortable in saying, *Thank you, God.*

He didn't have far to walk. Not far down the beach, the small boat he had already arranged for waited for him.

∼

With Clarin in bed, Tyler and Rebecca cuddled on the couch together in front of the fire. The warmth of the fire on his face made him sleepy. "I am glad to be back, and winter looks just fine to me," he said to his wife as he pulled her closer. He stroked her hair, and felt sleep overcoming him, but Rebecca had other ideas.

She kissed him, one long wonderful kiss, and then she leaned back and smiled at him. What did she have in mind? She kissed him again and he felt her fingers unbuttoning his shirt. She slipped it off, and ran her fingers over his chest. Then she started on the straps that kept his prosthesis on, he shrugged his shoulders to help her, and then they melted into each other.

The next morning, Tyler waited at the kitchen table. "You have that look," Tyler said as he watched his wife cook his eggs, over easy, just like he liked them.

"What do you mean, that look?"

"You want to tell me something. Why don't you just say it?"

"Well, there is something." She took a deep breath. "The recital went really well. Lot's of people in town are proud of Clarin and excited about her opportunities in life."

"I'm happy about that, but it's nothing new. We've all known, being a small town, that Clarin has something special. And I get it that the recital was special. I'm sorry I couldn't make it, but I'm certainly aware and happy about our daughter's gift."

"I know you are, darling, and I am really glad to have you home."

"I know what's coming. As short a time as I've been home, I've already had two women talk to me about special lessons for Clarin, which means probably the whole community is talking about it and wondering if we can afford the lessons. Am I right?"

"Yes, you're right. And no one is insinuating that we can't take care of our own and pay our own bills. It's just such an unusual gift our daughter has, and such an unusual and large expense, these music lessons."

"And what does her music teacher say?"

"Well, I have to give her credit. She is honest, as much as she loves Clarin, she thinks Clarin will need more than she has to offer."

"How soon?"

"Soon, and she has already recommended a teacher in Landing."

"Landing? Could be worse. Like Seattle." Tyler sighed. He looked at his wife, and in her loveliness and earnestness, he could see that she was tired. They both worked hard, and he appreciated what diligent care she took of their home, their family, and the bookkeeping of their business.

As for himself, he was tired of the outdoors and the cold he could feel in his own body. Maybe he was developing some arthritis. Working in the woodshop, with the heat cranked up, sounded awfully good to him.

"Tyler, her music teacher is so nice, and she just wants to be helpful. I love it that she cares so much for her students. She could just soak us for money and lessons, and I, darling, must admit I don't know much about music, and that could happen. Her music teacher is really a gem."

"So, who in Landing does she see our beautiful daughter getting appropriate music lessons from, seeing as how we live in the middle of nowhere and there can't be many options?"

"She actually has a retired friend, who lives there, and might be helpful. Might be very helpful."

"And this person teaches in Landing? Landing isn't that much bigger than Crystal."

"This gentleman used to play with the New York Symphony, and he doesn't teach, but he would likely be interested in Clarin, according to her teacher here."

"She's four-years-old, Rebecca. There's time. We don't have to rush. She needs to experience life as a four-year-old, and maybe a five-year-old before we get into something so heavy duty."

Rebecca put his breakfast in front of him and sat down. "I don't want us to have an argument over this. I'm just so glad your home now. I'm looking forward to the holidays and winter."

He knew she meant it, but he also knew she wasn't through with the topic, and it bothered him, the tiredness in her eyes.

"Are you feeling okay?" he asked as he started to eat.

She nodded yes. "I like it that so many people are interested and supportive of Clarin. It's almost like what I see in other towns, when a boy becomes a star on the high school football team. It brings the town together. In Landing, they're still talking about Rob McKinney and that 95-yard run he made for a touchdown five years ago."

"What's good ol' Rob doing now?"

"Getting ready to graduate from college. He's going to be a chemical engineer."

"And our daughter, at the age of four, is doing that for Crystal? Seems like people ought to get their own lives going." Tyler continued eating, but he could see, his wife wasn't through talking. And she did continue.

"It's just sort of amazing, Tyler, how much joy this town is getting out of our daughter and this situation. It seems like everybody in town wants to be helpful, even the newer people. Joanne and Ellen — they are new, but it's amazing how captivated they are and how helpful they want to be. They are the nicest people and so excited about Clarin and her talent. They aren't trying to be busybodies. They just care. They are just excited." She looked imploringly at Tyler. "Joanne is, after all, Andy's cousin."

"None of these people are us, though, and Rebecca, we make our own decisions about our own family."

"I know it. Now you're angry with me."

"What is it you want me to do?"

"I just think that the deal Ellen is offering you, one stressful day, would bring in lots of extra money. Money we could set aside for Clarins' education."

Tyler looked at his wife, young and earnest, and thought about Ellen and her daughter-in-law. They came across as the most pleasant people on the planet, but he was uncomfortable with them. Andy's cousin, Joanne, was another one — well-meaning but too pushy. *But I've got to do what is right, even if it looks like I've been pushed into it. I will not be pushed around by the women in the town when it comes to our daughter, but I will also not avoid doing the right thing, just to prove I've made my own decisions. Rebecca and I are the parents. Clarin is our daughter.*

Rebecca cleared her throat and then said, "Ellen wants to talk to you in the morning. She said she really does want to stay out of our business, but she does need to talk to you."

"I'll talk to her. But I'm feeling ganged up on and I don't like it. I'll go check on Deet and the horses." He hated to be at odds with his wife, but he hated it when other women took so much interest in her, and decided she needed steering. Clarin would do fine without expensive piano lessons, and he would find a way to barter for the wood he needed for the table he wanted to put in the governor's mansion. It was a chance of a lifetime and he could do it without some hair-brained scheme of a couple of women he didn't know.

Tyler headed for the solace of his barn, and found Deet shoeing a horse.

"Make your decision yet?" asked Deet as he peered up from where he was bent over the horse's back leg.

"No, I don't know what to do. What I do know is this. Everything seemed fine before people started pushing me to get Clarin some expensive piano lessons. They act like I'm abusing my child if I don't do it right away, before she gets old, *at four-years-old.*"

"Watch out for greed. It will get you every time. If you want to help, go look at the black gelding's hooves. Might need a real good picking."

Tyler went into the pasture and just stood, admiring the beauty of the black gelding, the peacefulness of the pasture and the rest of the horses grazing. He took the carrot out of his pocket and slowly approached the horse. The gelding came for his treat; Tyler got a firm grip on his mane and guided him over to the fence. Tyler picked up a rope lying on the fence, tied the horse securely, and bent over the back hoof, picking it up and looking at it. He went all around the horse, checking his feet, unaware that one of the chickens had followed him down to the pasture, and while Tyler was checking the gelding's last hoof, the chicken clucked loudly in front of the horse and caused him to spook and knock Tyler to the ground.

Surprised and dismayed to find himself in the dirt, Tyler looked up at the horse, and was even more irritated to see Deet looking down at him.

"Didn't I always teach you to be aware of what the horse is looking at?" asked Deet.

"Well, yeah. And I admit I never saw the chicken."

Deet gave him a hand up. "Always be aware of what's going on around you. Remember that. And a horse is a 1000-pound animal that doesn't care what you are looking at or thinking. You may think he cares, with those big brown eyes. *But he doesn't.*"

"Like some women."

"I don't want to hear about your love woes. Just remember what I said. I presume you want to stay out of the hospital for the rest of your life."

Tyler nodded and dusted himself off.

The next morning Tyler, as he agreed to do, met Ellen at the local coffee shop. They sat in a corner and ordered coffee.

"I have not been completely honest with you, and I need to do that, but I need to keep what is said here between you and me totally private," said Ellen.

"I don't usually keep things from my wife."

"You'll understand after I've talked."

He hesitated and then said, "Just tell what you need to tell me."

"Sally and I aren't really about planning an art outing. It's the iridium. I work for a pharmaceutical company that specializes in minerals and alternate uses for them. We have reason to believe that a meteor hit the mountain that your north fork path walks around, and that left an enormous deposit of iridium."

"Oh, come on. Next you're going to tell me 'There's gold in them thar hills,' or oil for the whole world. *Come on.*"

"I'm serious about this, Tyler. I'm dead serious. The research on this is behind closed doors, but looking promising, just like oil did years ago. And research in anything that helps health issues is expensive, and takes years and close to a billion dollars to bring to market. But some people, myself included, are involved. We dedicate years of our lives to something we hope will help other people. Change the world."

"And what is your plan for this iridium if it exists?" This was sounding farfetched to him.

"That it can help in treating cancer. Not cure cancer, but help in the treatment. We are in the final stages of another set of tests that show a definite link between the iridium and several cancers. This will be big news –- and we want to check out the validity of iridium deposits here before these test results are finalized. Let me repeat –- this will be a terrific and world-wide important discovery, and that is why I am so secretive."

"What's the name of your company?"

"I can't tell you that. The testing is already in progress, this isn't a joke or a scam. It looks more than promising. Almost a sure thing. Testing has been going on for years. And when I say years, I'm talking about decades. This is looking promising for the world. A geologist that works for us has been flying over this part of the country looking for iridium deposits and that's why I'm here. We want to get a handle on the possibilities before the news breaks to the rest of the world." She looked at him expectantly.

He needed to stall for time. What was happening here? "Tell me again, why are you so sure there is iridium up there?"

"A geologist who works for us has been flying over this part of the country, taking pictures, and studying the area. He is convinced about the meteor. This is not guesswork. We are talking scientific here. The meteor hit about 50,000 years ago. He knows how to read the pictures. The land formations tell a story. His scientific diagrams of the area are amazing. This is not a lightweight thing we're dealing with here. Lots of effort and commitment have been made to locate a source of iridium, and we have put a great deal of money at risk in pursuing this. The tests are looking so good, and my company wants to get a head start on the potential mother lode of iridium here. There may not be a deposit this big anywhere else in North America. Everything is legal and on solid ground, but you can't hold it against us, that after all we've done in this area of research, we want a head start on a possible mother lode. Can you? Of course, what my company is and what we are doing — I can't tell you that. This is top secret. But I have told you why it is so important that I make this hike now and not wait for spring. It will be one day that will pay you very well."

"This is a lot for me to swallow, and I'm not sure what to make of it."

"What do you have to lose? The money I will give you will more than make just a little difference to your family. It's enough to be life changing, and you will, whether you know it or not, be making a huge contribution to the well-being of the world. Cancer is a devastating disease, and this will be the biggest discovery in years to make headwinds against cancer. Join the team, Tyler. We've all taken risks, my company in particular. I'm just a lightweight in a company of scientists who have given their lives, taken a chance on this discovery and the help it will bring. Some have only worked on this for their whole careers."

"Let me think about it a minute."

It would be one long day. Deet would take them up to the campsite and they would hike from there, not a fun hike, and then down, down to the beach. He would have Deet meet them on the beach, if the tide was out -- it would be dark by then, and then Deet would drive them back to Crystal. If the tide was in, Deet would have to get them with a boat. Sounded simple, but Tyler knew it would not be easy. But, why not do that? Help Ellen get her samples, get out of there, and then he would have made a lot of money, provided better for his family, and then he would be through being a guide until spring. He would have money for the sideboard in the governor's mansion, and that opportunity would further his prospects in the business of woodworking. He would do it. The story sounded a bit far-fetched to him, but what did he know of such things? The world always sounded far-fetched to him. He would do it. He didn't like the thought that the women in town would congratulate themselves for his doing it, but that couldn't be helped. He did, however, need to talk money first.

"What kind of money are we talking about?" Tyler asked.

She replied quickly, and he made a low whistle. Worthwhile, indeed.

"I'll do it," he said. "But we leave early morning, day after tomorrow. There's a storm coming in off the Pacific, and it will likely bring snow. I aim to be out of there before the snow flies in the mountains., and you need to be sure you can carry everything you will need. Your tools for soil samples, food, water, and anti-bear spray. Get me some anti-bear spray while you're at it. The hardware store carries it."

"Which hardware store?" she asked.

"There's only one."

"Right! Got that. Thank you for taking this on. You won't regret it." She smiled at him, a most engaging smile.

"And wear layers," he said.

"Sure. Will do. This is wonderful!" she said. "I'll be ready. I'll get us both the anti-bear spray. Thank you very much. And here's your down payment." She pulled an envelope out of her purse and handed it to him.

He looked in, ran his thumb over the bills, and whistled again.

Tyler walked into the house with a big grin. He picked up his wife and swung her around and then put her down.

"What? What's going on?" asked Rebecca. "Tell me quick, what happened?"

Tyler looked around, and assured that Clarin was busy with her train set, he pulled out his wallet and proceeded to count out the large bills for his wife.

She looked on with amazement. "I am stunned. I didn't think it would be this much."

"That is only half. I'm taking Ellen and Sally." He decided not to tell her the rest.

She threw her arms around him and kissed him passionately. "Thank you. I know you are tired and ready for winter. Thank you."

"The snow could fly any day now. So we are going day after tomorrow. It will take us all day, with Deet taking us to the campsite. He'll pick us up on the beach after dark."

"Thank you. I know this will put a financial base under us for the next few years. Not only for Clarin's needs, but also the baby."

"The baby? Are you pregnant?"

"Yes, dearest."

He took her gently in his arms and was quiet for a long time. "I can't believe it," he said. "I'm so happy to be Clarin's father, that was enough for me. This blessing, this incredible blessing. I don't know what to say. Are you feeling okay?"

"I'm tired, but I'm okay. I haven't been to the doctor yet, but I am pregnant. Let's not tell anyone for a while. Okay?"

He took her in his arms again. "I hate to leave you, even for a day. You are one beautiful, wonderful woman." He kissed her gently.

Later, in the middle of the night, Tyler awoke with a start. He could see Rebecca's face was close to his, pale and looking worried. "Why so much money for an art retreat?" she asked.

"I have no idea. Wealthy women spend money in ways I don't understand." He would not tell her about the science part of the expedition until much later. It had seemed a little farfetched to him until he saw the cash, but cold hard cash had made a believer out of him, and he would protect their secret for now. Fighting cancer, looking for resources to do it — he would participate in that and keep their secret. And his family would benefit.

Rebecca curled up next to him. He could feel the warmth of her body and he marveled at life, the baby growing inside her. *What is it about church that I really don't like? What could be bigger or greater or show God more than what my wife and I have in this house? I like Andy, and know he is a blessing in my life, but I can't get interested in his church, when I have what I have here. And I know that God is here.*

∽

In the barn, Tyler talked to Deet while Deet shod a horse.

"So you'll be by at four in the morning. I'll have my gear ready. We'll pick up Ellen and Sally, head out and be up at the campsite by eight and you'll meet us on the beach at the end of our adventure at eight. Tide will be in. Sorry."

"I got it. Never will you have worked so little for so much money."

"Yeah, I know. I'm getting happier all the time with the deal."

Tyler went by the store to get the bear spray — he didn't trust Ellen to do it, but they were out. *Good girl, she's already bought it.*

∽

It was in hauling the last load of drapes out to the curb that the bright idea hit her. The main large room would also need to accommodate a piano or keyboard or other instruments for the singing that usually accompanies a worship service, and why not get Sally, and the art club members, to make some suggestions about how to arrange the room. Everyone seemed so excited about the house, why not get them involved? The excitement about Clarin, the house, the upcoming holidays — why not get more people involved? *Why not do it tonight?* Do it spontaneously and that way she would be relieved of cooking or providing anything extraordinary.

Joanne fixed herself a glass of tea and sat down to make the calls. Within half an hour's time, everything was arranged. Six women from the art club were coming -- including three people who knew something about music, Clarin's music teacher, Sally, and herself.

The first guest arrived promptly at seven o'clock, and within ten minutes of her arrival, everyone else was there and gathered within the parlor.

Joanne had tea and cookies ready for them. They all wandered around the lower floor of the house and remarked how it was starting to sparkle. They talked, the old-timers, of the last time they had been in the house. Joanne got them settled into the great room and then guided their thoughts.

"Can you picture this? The room filled with forty or fifty people, how it needs to look? Where to put the piano? I need your ideas. It will help me get the report I'm writing ready for Andy. What color would you recommend he paint the walls?"

What a happy, friendly group. They laughed and talked and Joanne took notes. Not everything would work. She would write up the plan later, but for now she wrote it all down and enjoyed the group, their knowledge about color, and what was needed for the town -- it was a grand experience. And of course, some of the conversation veered to Tyler's adventure with Ellen and Sally, but anytime she could, Sally tried to modestly change the subject.

Joanne liked that about her. Every day she felt more and more like she was part of a family in this little town. Every day she found something she liked, that was admirable and pleased her. And even though she knew better than to say something about Clarin and her talent, she was so happy to have helped a little bit in encouraging Tyler. No need to make a deal out of it, but she was a part of something grand happening, not just for this town, but for that dearest little girl's future. It was healing that part of her that felt so devastated about her marriage and her daughter. It all had drifted into the background.

At home that night, Tyler put Clarin to bed with a story about walking in the woods and there were elves in the woods. The elves didn't look friendly at first. They pulled tricks on people who walked through the forest and scurried from one tree to another, hard to see and hard to understand. But then the elves started to talk to the big people who came walking through the forest. Clarin giggled and hid under the covers.

"What are they going to do to the big people?" asked Clarin.

"I think they're going to tickle the big people," said Tyler as he grabbed his daughter and tried to tickle her. She screamed and dove deeper into the bed covers.

"I think you're getting her awake rather than putting her to bed," said Rebecca from the door.

Tyler grabbed his daughter and kissed her and then they said a prayer together. *Dear Father, Thanks for this day, for taking care of us, and thank you for Jesus. Amen.*

"Goodnight, kiddo. Do as Mama says and go to sleep."

"Goodnight, Daddy. I love you."

He started for the door, but turned around. "I love you, too, sweetness."

He started for the door again and got all the way to the door when he heard, "Daddy, are elves real?"

"No. Go to sleep. Now. Or your mother will come in here and tell you to stay awake all night. That won't be any fun!"

She giggled and snuggled deeper into the blankets.

Tyler pulled the door closed and went in search of his wife. He found her in bed.

"Wow, are you feeling bad?" he asked.

"Just tired. It feels good to be here. Want to join me?"

"I'm ready for tomorrow, so give me a few minutes to brush my teeth and I'm with you!"

When he returned to the bedroom, she was sound asleep, her beautiful hair splayed out on the pillow. He was only temporarily disappointed. He climbed into the bed and kissed her cheek, admiring her beauty. Then he lay down, put his arm around her, and soon he was asleep.

He awoke at 3:30 in total darkness, and got out of bed without waking his wife. He looked forward to the day, and he looked forward to it being over. He didn't like having money he hadn't yet earned.

∽

When Deet and Tyler rolled up in front of the motel where Sally and Ellen were staying, it all looked dark and Tyler worried. But Ellen immediately stepped out with her backpack and climbed in the truck.

"Where's Sally?" asked Tyler.

"She's not feeling well. I can do this and maybe you and I will actually move along faster. She likes to stop and admire every leaf and flower. I hate to criticize her, though. She's a wonderful daughter-in-law."

What does it matter to me, thought Tyler. *We'll move faster without her.* Deet took off and the three were silent, admiring the early morning beauty.

The road wound around and then Deet took a right turn onto a poorly paved road. It then turned into a gravel road. The sky started to lighten. Deet finally pulled into the campsite. The shelter looked gloomy and dark.

"It all looks better when there's a fire going and Deet has something good cooking," said Tyler.

"I can imagine," said Ellen. "You have the people riding up, and then Deet is already here, with all the comforts taken care of. Smart plan. Experience the west, without the strain. I'll come another day and do that."

They unloaded their gear and strapped it on.

"Tide will be in so I'll be there with a boat," said Deet.

"What? No walk in the dark on the beach? That's actually fine with me," said Ellen. She stood ready. Tyler appreciated that. She knew how to deal with her pack without a lot of help from him.

Tyler pointed the way, but then asked Ellen. "Did you get that bear spray?"

"No," said Ellen. "The store was out. Will it be a problem?"

"No. We'll be careful. It'll be okay." Tyler wondered about that, but then he didn't know what every guide in town was doing. They would be okay. The bears wouldn't bother them if they weren't bothered first. The bears were more interested in getting themselves fed and prepared for winter. But still, bears were not to be taken lightly. *They needed to be careful.*

"I'll stay here until you're out of sight," said Deet. "Then I'll be back on the beach in the dark. Don't expect me to be coming up that hill to help at that point. I'll be on the beach. With a boat."

Tyler started down the path, taking down some limbs as he proceeded down the overgrown path. Ellen kept her distance. Tyler could see he wouldn't have to babysit her. This would go all right.

Tyler heard Deet's truck start and then move down the road. Deet and he worked together hand in glove. Tyler still had a bit of uneasiness, about what he didn't know. But Deet always gave him space and comfort, all at the same time. He had learned a lot from the old timer, and felt privileged to know him. An old-timer, with a good work ethic, lots of sense, and once in a while, Deet would say something that amazed Tyler with his wisdom and understanding of people.

Ellen followed Tyler without talking much or complaining. They had hiked for forty-five minutes when she said, "Wait!" Tyler turned around and she pointed at a rock formation. He nodded and waited while she took off her pack, took a sample of the rocks and soil, and then put the pack back on. They continued, with her stopping them several more times. At one point she stumbled, and Tyler quickly went back to help her.

"Thank you," she said. "But I've got it."

And she did. She picked herself up, brushed herself off, and continued on.

"I wish all the people, men and women, that I had to deal with were as positive and self-reliant as you are," said Tyler.

"You are a man of few words, and so I take the compliment seriously," said Ellen. "Is your wife into horses and hiking?"

"She's more of a homebody, but she likes being outdoors. She just likes being inside when the sun goes down."

"I get that," said Ellen. "Not a bad way to be."

"I'm getting that way more, the older I get."

She nodded.

"What will you do with the money you earn from this adventure? Besides the music lessons?"

"I'll make a special table, a sideboard, for the governor's mansion. I've been invited to do that."

"Wow. That'll be great advertising. Good for you."

She didn't complain and she wanted to do her part. He liked that about her. Tyler wished all the women he dealt with were this knowledgeable and easy to get along with. Often his female clients, the major part of his business, were quick to complain about bugs, blisters, and other traumas, demanding a stop, time and attention.

"Are you ready for food soon?" asked Tyler.

"Any time you say."

Tyler found an old stump to use as a table, and they stopped.

"The trees are magnificent. Do you ever get tired of this?" asked Ellen.

"I never get tired of trees. I can easily get tired of people, testy horses, and bad movies, but I never get tired of beautiful trees."

Ellen got her own pack off easily without asking for help.

Joanne didn't remember when she had been this happy — happy with her work, happy in this place, and happy in her personal relationships. Somehow her life in Colorado had filled with people who were less than what they should be, and she could see here in Crystal that people could be different. Everywhere she went, there were encounters with people that were caring and down-to-earth, and of course they all knew that Tyler, with the support of Rebecca, who obviously didn't feel well, was going the extra mile to ensure that Clarin's music lessons would be taken care of. Just as a high school athlete in a small town can bring a town together and bring pride to everyone, Clarin, at four-years-old was doing that with music. Joanne liked that. It was time, after all, for the world to notice such things of culture and beauty and for football to recede a little bit. It was all so special. So sweet. So grand to be a part of it all.

Joanne busied herself cleaning the great room. The meeting the previous night had not been large, but still it created its own cleaning job. She vacuumed the floors and the couches. The couches would have to go, after all, but until they did, she would clean them and clean them often. It was while fluffing the pillows that Joanne found the wallet. A woman's wallet for sure. It must have slipped out of a purse of one of the women from yesterday's meeting. She picked it up, put it on the table and completed her work on the sofa. She hated to be nosey, but she needed to look in the wallet, so she'd know to whom to return it. She picked it up and turned it to see the window meant for the driver's license. She recognized the picture of Sally, but not the name on the license. She double-checked the picture. It sure looked like Sally, but the last name was Reinquist.

Reinquist? Joanne was terrible with names, but she was sure Sally had introduced herself as Sally Jones. Maybe Sally James. But not Reinquist. Of that much, she was absolutely certain.

Joanne took the wallet, careful to not peek at anything else, and put it on the kitchen counter. She knew Sally was out on the trail with Ellen and Tyler today, so Joanne would keep it safe until they got back.

She continued with her work until lunchtime, and then she would go to town and treat herself to a bacon burger at the Mountain View Café. She hummed as she worked. She could see why Andy wanted a church in this town. It was so special, so full of caring people.

I wish Larry and Jasmine could see me here. I wish they could see how beautiful a simple loving community can be. Andy was so right. Dear sweet, loving Andy. He was so wise. He knew I needed to be here, to put all this love on me in the community. I will thank him by doing the best possible job getting this house ready. This beautiful, wonderful house.

~

"Are you doing okay?" asked Tyler. He couldn't hear Ellen's answer, so he turned around to look.

"Getting tired?" he asked her.

"Yes, indeed. But I will finish this assignment. No way out but through, right?"

"That's right. I'll slow the pace a bit. Do you need any soil samples here?"

"No, not here. I'll let you know."

She had her head down and was keeping on.

"What are you thinking about?" asked Tyler as she caught up with him.

"I'm thinking about literally putting one foot in front of another and keeping my eye on the soil around me, and that's it. No wonder you were reluctant to do this in one day."

On the trail, Ellen and Tyler continued on their trek. Tyler could tell Ellen was starting to move a little slower and so he slowed the pace. This was where they needed to be more conscious of safety. This is where they didn't need an accident.

"Entertain me with some bear stories?" asked Ellen as they hiked.

"Sure. First of all, they are basically going to leave us alone, but they can be dangerous, especially if we are between a bear and his food, or we get between a mother and her cubs. They are preparing for winter right now, so they are pretty cranky about the food."

"Did you ever have one attack you?"

"I have surprised several and attack was imminent. None got their hands on me. One time I was exploring a trail by myself, much like we are doing today, and found I had walked, lost in my own thoughts, mind you, right between a napping bear and his kill, a nice buck. It got ugly fast."

"What happened?"

"The bear chased me. I stumbled and thought it was all over. But the bear spray, it saved me. The bear took off, and I was pretty miserable with the stuff myself. But I'm here to tell about it."

"Sorry I wasn't able to get some bear spray."

Tyler did not reply. They kept walking.

"You really haven't heard story-telling until you've heard Deet around a campfire," said Tyler.

"Tell me about Deet," said Ellen as she stopped, took off her backpack and knelt to take more soil samples.

"Deet looks old, but he is one strong, competent woodsmen, horsemen, and deputy sheriff."

"I have to admit, he looks pretty worn."

"He's a great shot, too. When he goes hunting, he makes his kill."

"Did somebody tell me that he used to work on boats? How did you meet him?"

Tyler waited until Ellen was ready to go forward again, and then talked about how Deet emerged in his life through a mutual friend, Collin Matthews. Ellen didn't seem to be listening as much.

∽

Joanne stepped in to the cafe. The breakfast crowd was waning. Grace, the waitress called out, "Joanne! Come sit here by the window. Great place for you."

Joanne slid into the booth. "How are you, Grace? How's your mother? That was a nasty fall she had."

Grace, in her rhinestone jeans and striped shirt, looked very spiffy for a woman in her fifties. She leaned against the booth, taking a little break to talk to Joanne.

"My mother is such a cranky person, she doesn't know how lucky she is to have me, and I appreciate your asking about her. Let me tell you, it's those two stupid dogs that she's gaga about. They are so ill-mannered, and she got into a mess trying to take them on a walk. I'm sure it looked funny, if it hadn't been so serious, scary, and potentially life-changing for her."

Joanne smiled at the picture of the whole thing. "Where is she now? Or more importantly, where are the dogs?"

"She's home. And she is mad at me. The dogs aren't there. They're with me, little twerps. She didn't break anything, but she needs to heal and not have any more of their antics. And, of course, I'm waiting on her hand and foot, when I'm not here. And, of course, taking care of the stupid dogs."

"I'd be glad to stop by and check on her, if you think that will be helpful," said Joanne.

"Love it. I'll be right back to get your order. If you could stop in the middle of the afternoon, that would help. And did you know Rebecca is pregnant? We will all need to keep track of her. She will need some help."

Joanne nodded at this news, pleased to know, to be included. She ordered coffee and a cheeseburger, and smiled, smiled at nothing in particular but everything in general. Colorado seemed far away, she was happy in the moment in this place, doing a good deed for her cousin, and already feeling like she was important in this town. *I am accepted here. No one knows of my distressing year, my failures.*

Her favorite waitress, Chloe, was old, and moved with tiny slow steps like Tim Conway used to on the Carol Burnett show. That show was years ago, but still funny in Joanne's mind. What was the name of the character that Conway played? Chloe's mind was still sharp and she was a thoughtful person. Joanne watched Chloe and Grace move through the café in their own individual way, their own effective dance.

CHAPTER 8

Rebecca melted into the sofa with a huge sigh. Tyler kissing her goodbye, that seemed like a dream so long ago. She put her head back and loved the feel of the support on every part of her body. *It isn't that I'm tremendously nauseated, but that I am so tired. What could I have been thinking, getting pregnant again? Why didn't I wait, like until Clarin was going to college? How can I do this and take care of Clarin, and Tyler, and our lives? Probably I should have waited until Clarin was out of school, having her own babies, and then I, also with a newborn could sneak my baby into her nursery, saying, "Clarin. You're young, so much smarter and stronger than I, you don't mind, do you?"*

"The train is going to town to get the people..." Rebecca didn't listen to the rest of Carin's game. The battery-run train stopped and started often as it struggled to stay on the tracks. Clarin, patient, coaxed it and its crew to get to town to the people. *Stay on the tracks, and go get the people.*

Tired from the very core of her being, Rebecca closed her eyes, knowing that she couldn't sleep; she had to stay awake and keep track of Clarin. Clarin sat peacefully on the rug in front of the sofa, but Rebecca knew that Clarin could quickly decide to get something important for the train, and therefore head to another room, like the kitchen for that all-important thing. When Clarin needed to do something, she wanted to do it immediately. And of course, when Clarin got bored, Clarin moved fast. The train game could quickly become something else.

Rebecca couldn't help it. She leaned over and curled up on the couch. Clarin continued playing with her train and Rebecca thought, I can shut my eyes for a little bit. I can doze off and get a little rest. I will hear her if she moves away. She succumbed to that thought and dozed off, but then became aware of something different. She opened her eyes and stared directly into Clarin's eyes. Rebecca, startled, blinked.

"I'm sorry, Mommy. Did I scare you?"

"I guess so, baby."

"Are you sick, Mommy?"

"Just tired, Clarin."

"I'll be your doctor and you'll get better." Clarin's solemn eyes stared at her mother, and Rebecca decided this was the answer. She could let Clarin play doctor, she would know exactly where Clarin was, and therefore get a brief nap.

"Yes, go get your doctor kit from your bedroom," said Rebecca.

Clarin darted from the room and within seconds returned from her bedroom, put her kit on the coffee table, and then opened it and studied the contents. "Where do you hurt, Mommy?"

"All over."

"Okay, I'll listen first."

Clarin used her stethoscope and proceeded to listen to Rebecca's body, wherever the blanket didn't cover her, her neck, her arm, her one exposed leg.

Rebecca dozed. Clarin chattered on about the illnesses in each body part.

Clarin decided Rebecca's wrist needed a splint, and took quite a few minutes to do that.

Once again, instead of drifting into deep sleep, Rebecca reluctantly opened her eyes; she saw Clarin staring at her.

"Does your face hurt, Mommy?"

Not really, but Rebecca answered, "Yes."

Clarin asked, "Do you need bandages on your face?"

Rebecca contemplated that only briefly. "Yes, of course."

Through half-closed eyes, Rebecca watched Clarin retrieve a box of tissues from the coffee table, kneel by her mother, and start tearing the tissue into little pieces. She took a piece and put it on her mother's face. It didn't stick, so Clarin put the piece gently on her own tongue, just barely moistening it, and then put it on her mother's face.

Rebecca didn't know how long this game would last, but took the opportunity to drift off again. Over and over Clarin put little bandages on her mother's face and Rebecca dozed on, half awake, half asleep, but getting some rest, not caring what her face might look like, and enjoying her little girl's sweet nature.

∼

Joanne hummed to herself as she tidied up the kitchen and finished her chores. *I can't believe how peaceful it is to be here in this town, and be a part of it. I wish my daughter and my ex-husband could see me here. And what an extra blessing to be a part of Tyler, Rebecca, and Clarin's lives. This little girl will have a stunning life, partly because I gently helped steer this situation. Surely it was part of God's plan that I be here, doing more than taking care of the house.*

Joanne didn't bother locking the door as she set off to check on Grace's mother and then Rebecca and Clarin. When she reached her first destination, she found Grace's mother, Kathy, peacefully reading a book and not in need of anything, so Joanne cheerfully said goodbye and moved on.

Maybe there was something she could do more for Rebecca and Clarin, with Tyler gone on his adventure. She felt like she was powered by the sun rays bouncing off the side walk. She stopped to admire a baby in a stroller and chat with the mother. Then she helped an elderly gentleman get out of his car and up the steps to his house.

Humming joyfully, Joanne continued to Rebecca's house and opened the gate, seeing nothing of the little girl and her mother. The house looked strangely quiet. *What if they're taking a nap?* Joanne hated to ring the doorbell. She decided instead to knock quietly, and indeed, she heard Rebecca call through the door, "Come in."

Joanne quietly opened the door and saw Rebecca lying on the sofa and Clarin playing beside her. Clarin smiled at Joanne. *What a delightful child.*

Joanne walked in and sat down on the floor beside Clarin. "What are you doing, you two?"

"I'm the doctor and Mommy is the patient," said Clarin.

"Yes, well, good for you. What exactly is Mommy's illness?" asked Joanne, looking curiously at the tiny pieces of paper attached to Rebecca's face.

Rebecca yawned and then said, "These are bandages, bandages on wounds of unknown origin."

"I'm helping Mommy feel lots better," said Clarin. "I'm her doctor and I'm doing a good job."

"I have no doubt about that," said Joanne. She looked closer at Rebecca's eyes. She could see the fatigue and assumed the rumors were true and that Rebecca was pregnant. What to do now? The joy of the whole situation was tempered by serious need, and it was always Joanne's desire to help in times of serious need.

"What can I do to help you?" asked Joanne as she looked at the scene. Clarin just glanced at her once, preferring to keep at her task.

"I need to sleep so much, and I promised Deet I would take him a sandwich for lunch. Clarin and I usually do that this time of day."

"How about I take Clarin over to the barn for a little walk. I'll keep her safe, give Deet his sandwich, and bring Clarin home. I'll play with her in the next room until you wake up."

"Joanne, you are such a blessing. I'm so glad you came to our community, and yes, that sounds like a wonderful plan. Your daughter was lucky to have you. I'm so glad she has shared you with us."

Joanne didn't know what to say. *If you only knew, my daughter doesn't see me that way at all.*

"Come here, baby," Rebecca said to Clarin. Rebecca held Clarin's face in her hand. "I want you to go with Joanne and mind her and be very safe, do you hear me?"

"Yes, Mama."

"You are going to do with her exactly what you and I have done many times. Take Deet a sandwich. You mind her, understand?"

"Can I feed the chickens?"

"Yes, but don't get into that coup. No running back and forth in the chicken coup. And you mind Joanne. Do you hear?"

Clarin nodded and Rebecca sank back on the sofa, closing her eyes.

Joanne opened the refrigerator and asked Clarin, who stood beside her, "What kind of sandwich does Deet like?"

"He likes any old thing Mama takes him," said Clarin.

"Got that. I see some leftover chicken in here. What do you think?"

Clarin nodded and together they made a chicken salad sandwich.

"What else should we take Deet?" asked Joanne. "I see some cake on the counter."

"Nope. Deet doesn't like cake. Just a sandwich."

"Odd man," said Joanne to herself, but Clarin heard her.

"Daddy says he's a great oddity and a great blessing."

"I wouldn't argue with your dad about that!"

"But we can take some old lettuce for the chickens, and a carrot for a horse."

She then helped Clarin get her jacket on and took her hand. They walked the two blocks, stopping to say hello to one of the neighbors and stopping again to pet a black cat. Joanne opened the gate for both of them. She did not see any sign of Deet, but his truck was parked by the barn.

After Joanne and Clarin shut the gate, they turned around to see a pony walking determinedly toward them.

"What a cute pony," said Joanne.

"That's Cathy," said Clarin.

Cathy stopped in front of them, waiting for a treat.

Joanne reached out to touch Cathy's perfectly brushed flaxen mane and tail. She then pulled a carrot out of Deet's lunch bag, and she and

Clarin together carefully held it for Cathy, who looked at them with large, brown. appreciative eyes as she took the carrot. Clarin giggled when the pony's soft lips brushed her hand.

The chickens, seeing treats had arrived, rushed toward them clucking and moving their little legs as fast as they could. The five hens scurried around Clarin's feet as she tossed the little bits of lettuce that Joanne handed her. Clarin laughed and twirled while throwing out the little pieces of lettuce.

Cathy, satisfied with her treat, moved back to green grass, and Joanne watched Clarin feed and dance with the chickens until she remembered Deet and the sandwich. The sandwich was in danger of being donated to the chickens.

"Let's go over by the barn," said Joanne. She still didn't see Deet anywhere. She took Clarin by the hand and then walked to the barn door.

"I'll go in and find Deet," she said. "I want you to stay right here, and feed the chickens the rest of this lettuce. A little bit at a time. If you need me, just call. I'm just inside the barn. Okay?"

The chickens roamed around Clarin's feet and Clarin was mesmerized by them. Joanne left her by the door of the barn and entered. It took a few seconds for Joanne's eyes to adjust to the darkness, and she still saw nothing of Deet.

"Deet? Deet?" He did not respond.

The empty dark barn showed no sign of life, not even the resident shy cat. She walked over to the side and looked out. She could see the horses peacefully grazing. But no Deet.

Joanne walked back to the door and stairs that led up to Deet's apartment. She opened the door and yelled up the steps, "Deet?"

No answer. She couldn't see anything in the dark cavern of the stairwell. She backed out, and listened. She could still hear Clarin and the chickens. What if Deet was upstairs and sick? She needed to go up the stairs. It would only take a few seconds. Clarin was fine. She would go halfway up the stairs, and yell for Deet. Maybe he was mesmerized on his computer with something and didn't hear her. Her eyes had adjusted to the darkness of the steps and she saw something.

What was that laying on the stairs? A body! Was that Deet? Where was the light switch? Joanne stepped into the hallway and started to lean over the body when something wacked her on the back of her head. Blackness engulfed her, and then stars. Pain beyond anything she had ever felt before took her mind completely; she could not escape from it.

A noise, a scream -- Joanne had a faint realization it came out of her own throat.

I'm falling...I'm falling...I'm falling....

∼

Clarin liked the chickens, more than any other animals on Daddy's farm. The horses and the cows, they were too big. The chickens liked to be fed and they were smaller than her. She could chase them and no one yelled at her. And she liked looking at them -- their different colors and feathers. She had one piece of lettuce left, but left it in her pocket and was chasing them in circles when she heard her name.

"Clarin? Clarin?"

She stopped and turned around, expecting to see Joanne, but it was Sally, kneeling in the dirt, looking at the chickens.

"I like the chickens best of all," Sally said, looking at Clarin on the same level and smiling.

Clarin smiled back. Sally had a nice smile, full of sunshine.

"Do you want to feed the chickens, too?" asked Clarin.

"Sure," said Sally. She took a piece of lettuce that Clarin withdrew from her pocket and threw it on the ground. Two chickens started pecking at it, pecking at each other, fighting for the lettuce.

"My daddy says to give them each smaller pieces and then they won't fight," said Clarin.

"Indeed. I'll remember that next time."

Sally stood up and then said, "Joanne and Deet are busy. They want you to come with me."

"Where are we going?" asked Clarin.

"Just to run an errand. It will be a nice surprise for your mother. Wouldn't you like to get her a present?"

"Yes, what kind of present?"

"Let's get in the car, it's around the side of the barn, and we will go together and figure out a nice present for your mom. Okay?"

Clarin brushed the remaining bits of lettuce off her hands and smiled up at Sally. She put her hand in Sally's and they walked around the barn and got into Sally's car.

"This is a pretty car seat," said Clarin, looking at the pink cushion with horses all over it.

"Yes, it is. Brand new, too," said Sally.

Clarin watched Sally get in the driver's seat, lock the doors, and then they drove away from the barn. She did not see Joanne, but that was okay, Sally had a smile full of sunshine.

Sally handed a piece of candy to Clarin when they stopped at the gate. A red lollipop. After Sally had driven through the gate, locked it, and got back in the car, Clarin was happily into her heart-shaped sucker and getting sleepy. The car felt warm and the pretty car seat made her happy. Shopping for Mommy, that was exciting, but for now, she felt sleepy.

Sally drove slowly, to not cause any attention, but she carefully avoided the center of Crystal, and headed out of town. In the rearview mirror, she could see Clarin's precious head, her hair covering her face as she slept. *Precious, precious Clarin. Beautiful little girl. And now, my beautiful little girl. We will have a good life, a sweet life. You, your dad, and me. And let's not forget Grandma. You get a grandma in the bargain.*

~

"Joanne? Joanne? I know you're in there. I know you're not dead."

Deet shook Joanne gently. She did not move

"Joanne, wake up."

He pinched her cheek lightly and she stirred. She opened her eyes and looked at him questioningly. "What's going on and why does my head hurt so badly?"

"I think the same person who clobbered me got you. Why, I don't know. Can you get up?"

"I don't know. My head is killing me. I'll try."

Joanne sat up slowly. Deet helped her lean against the wall.

"Clarin!" she said.

"What?"

"Clarin! Where is she? I left her right at the door of the barn, feeding the chickens, when I stepped in here looking for you."

Deet stood up and walked to the barn door, rubbing the back of his head. He stopped at the door and looked around. The chickens peacefully scratched for food in the dirt. No Clarin. He walked around the side of the barn and saw only horses grazing peacefully. He circled all the way around the barn. No Clarin.

When he got back inside the barn, Joanne was standing, shakily holding onto the wall.

"She's not here," said Deet. "If she was here that old collie of mine would have tagged along with her, wherever she went. The dog is sleeping out front. Clarin is not here."

"You're sure she wouldn't walk down to the pasture to see the horses? Are you sure?"

"I'm sure. Positive. That Collie would never leave her. That dog has been lying out there in the sun."

"Maybe she walked home by herself. Oh, please God, let her be there. Please God."

"Come on, get up and get walking. I'll get my truck." *Oh, dear God, please let Clarin be safely at home. Please, please please don't let this be what it appears to be. Please.*

Deet brought his truck around and helped Joanne into it. Driving the two blocks took forever, in Deet's mind, although it actually only took seconds. Neither spoke as they got out and raced to the house. Joanne didn't knock, but opened the door and called out, "Rebecca? Rebecca? Where are you?'

They found her lying on the sofa, asleep.

Joanne knelt down beside her. "Rebecca? Wake up! Wake up!"

Rebecca opened her eyes and looked at both Joanne and then Deet. "What's happened? What are you doing here?" She sat up and looked around. "Where's Clarin?"

Joanne and Deet told her what happened and then the three of them raced through the house, shouting Clarin's name, looking into every private hiding place. When they were all three back in the living room, not knowing what to say, Deet finally spoke.

"It's likely a kidnapping, and it likely was Sally. She did not go with Tyler and me and Ellen this morning."

"That would make sense of the name. I found her wallet, and the picture on the license was Sally, but a different name. But why? Why?" asked Joanne.

"What name was on the driver's license?" asked Rebecca, her voice grave.

"Reinquist."

Rebecca's face froze in horror. "Oh, my God, please no." She buried her face in her hands.

"What's going on?" asked Deet.

"That name, that's the name of Clarin's biological father. Ellen must be his mother, but Sally, with that name, must be his wife. And Sally is married to him? Where is my daughter? *Where have they taken her?*"

CHAPTER 9

"It's getting dark. Do you have enough samples?" asked Tyler.

"I'm thinking that that rock formation up there is important."

What happened to the goodwill between us? Something's changed. I feel like she's stalling for time, and I don't know why. I just want to get out of here.

Tyler looked where she pointed, his impatience rising. He had been impressed with Ellen's efforts at first, but now, she seemed obsessive and he was ready to get out of the forest.

Ellen took out her camera and took pictures. Tyler watched as she put the camera away and started up the hill to the ledge. She took her samples and then slid back down the hill. Then she proceeded to pull a snack bar out of her backpack and sat down on a rock to eat it.

"Now, what do you think you're doing?" asked Tyler.

She smiled brightly at him, didn't answer, and continued eating. Finally, she brushed her hands free of crumbs, and stood up.

"I know what I'm talking about. And I know what I'm doing."

He did not respond. When she was ready, he started back on to the path, stopped, and insisted she go first. That lasted only a few minutes, and then she said, "I'm frightened. You have to go first."

He took the lead.

"Keep up. It's starting to get dark, and I hope you have what you came for." The unease in him was indefinable and unexplainable, but he knew he couldn't ignore it.

∽

A logging truck exploded? How could that be? All available officers and vehicles were on the way and so was Deet. Sort of. He had left Joanne to take care of Rebecca and organize a search around Crystal, and now Deet drove as fast as he could to the scene of the logging truck, a logging truck that had exploded and was burning on the highway south of Landing, blocking traffic both ways.

Only Deet knew he wasn't really headed there. He knew he had no time to go there, and try to convince the sheriff that he thought a kidnapping was in progress, and sheriff, can you spare me some men to go stop this thing? No. He was on his own. He needed to go to Landing and find Clarin. And he needed a boat. There had been no time to hook up Tyler's boat and trailer it to Landing.

Was that a coincidence? A traffic accident south of Landing. All hands-on deck except for Deet? Damn, he couldn't get the truck to moving any faster unless he wanted to cause an accident himself.

He had no help, but help would probably cause more problems. The way he saw it, they would try to escape by water. What else could make sense? But what did that mean? That meant that Ellen and Tyler would come out of the forest, and likely get on a boat already in that little bay. That had to mean Sally and the little girl were already on a boat out in that bay. *I don't understand this plan. I don't understand what they are doing there. I am only guessing. And I am pretty sure, that all things being what they look like, is that no way are they needing Tyler on that boat. Tyler is going to be left on that godforsaken trail. Dead.*

Deet headed for the marina.

"Yeah, that's right. I want to rent a little boat, that one right there," he said, pointing to a skiff. No point in trying to enlist help, maybe there were accomplices. *I intend to live through this.*

Deet didn't recognize the young man and therefore didn't want to raise any suspicions. He peeled out some cash and made sure the boat had plenty of gas.

"This engine, it don't take much gas and you can have a lot of fun for a day. That big boat that left this morning, now that's a different story."

"Tell me about that big boat," said Deet.

"It came in a couple of days ago, and a woman came in this morning and took it out. And filling that up cost her a pretty penny."

"Anybody with her?" asked Deet.

"I didn't see anybody. It was a man that brought it in, though."

∼

Joanne stood at the porch rail, unable to see through her tears. Rebecca was still in the bathroom, dealing with her own fear and grief.

I know I have made this situation worse. I know it. I know I didn't cause it. How could I have been so egotistical, to show up in this town and think I should have an opinion on things that I actually had no right to?

Joanne went to the bathroom and listened at the door. She could hear Rebecca praying. Good. Rebecca was not stupid. Joanne, maybe, but not Rebecca.

Joanne went back to the porch. How could she have been so stupid? This young woman had obviously gone through much trauma in life, but she, Joanne, had arrived, thinking she would be a big help, being much more mature and wise. She had worked to influence Tyler and Rebecca, and the awfulness of her own judgement, the arrogance of it, filled Joanne with disgust at herself.

"Joanne?"

Joanne turned to see Rebecca, composed, white-faced, standing in the doorway.

"I think we need a plan," she said.

"Of course." There was Rebecca, young, pregnant, distraught mother, looking wiser than Joanne had ever been.

"What do you suggest?" asked Joanne. *Nice. Good of you to ask. God, please let that little girl live. Please let Tyler live. Let all of them live to be reunited in the near future. Please God, forgive me for my arrogance, my trying to influence Tyler to take Ellen and Sally on the hike. My putting pressure on both Rebecca and Tyler to get more music lessons for Clarin. Clarin might still be here, with her mother and father looking after her, if I'd just left them alone in making their decisions.*

Joanne waited for Rebecca to speak, but Rebecca remained quiet as she let herself down into a chair on the porch.

"I have to trust that Deet is doing all he can, that he has alerted the authorities."

Joanne nodded.

"What we don't need is mass hysteria in town. But, in case, by any chance Clarin is in town, and wandered off, we need to find her. I don't think that's the case. I'm convinced of who these people are and what they want." She sighed.

"We don't know how many of them there are, and we don't want Tyler or Clarin in unnecessary danger. Would you go into town, and get a handful of volunteers who can comb the town, especially around the barn? I repeat, we don't need mass hysteria. Be sure they understand that."

Joanne nodded her head and immediately started for town, determined to do a good job. Determined, leaning on God, to keep the hysteria within herself, quiet. She walked as fast as she could through the neighborhood, into town, and to the best place in town to contact people. *The café.*

"Hi, hon. How's Rebecca?" asked Grace.

"Not so good. We've got a problem." She proceeded to tell her story. When she had finished, the waitress looked thoughtful only for a few seconds and then said. "I know exactly who we need to get on a search. Go back to Rebecca. I've got this. Take care of her."

Tyler led the way, listening carefully, knowing she was following him. He listened carefully to noises around them, the wind, while still gentle, created a low roar. He checked once in a while to see if she was still behind him. The clouds darkening the sky made it difficult for him to see.

He stopped and turned to Ellen. "We are almost to the turn where we head to the beach. It's a narrow path headed to the beach. It's the only path to the beach, due to the rugged coast, for many miles."

Ellen checked her watch, which Tyler thought odd, but no need to do anything now, but get them out of there. Getting down this path and to the beach where Deet would await them with his truck; that was enough. The path used to have built in wooden steps and a rough handrail down to the beach, but that had deteriorated long ago, and whatever shape it was in now would be quite hazardous. They couldn't hurry without taking unnecessary risks.

"I'm done. I appreciate your patience. I won't need to stop anymore."

Tyler nodded. "Come on. We're on the home stretch. Deet awaits."

They continued on the rough path, overgrown with tree branches and brush that whipped at their faces. The canopy of trees overhead seventy-five or more feet high, now darkened even more. The tops of the trees waved back and forth as the wind picked up. They rounded a corner and straight ahead stood a large black bear, ripping at the remnants of an animal.

Tyler's heart ceased beating at the surprise of it, the closeness of it, but the sheer power of the bear also added to the horror as it ripped at the carcass. Then, even more frightening — the bear stopped ripping at the carcass and glowered at Tyler and Ellen, throwing his head from side to side roaring. "Stand still!" said Tyler, knowing Ellen was behind him. The bear, not happy about the intruders on her buffet, watched them for a moment, and then went back to her meal but also staring at Tyler and Ellen. Tyler could feel his heart pounding against the wall of his chest. There was no other way down and out. The bear, directly blocking the path, took a step toward them.

"We could have used that bear spray right about now," said Tyler.

"I see that," she replied. "My apologies."

"Like that helps."

Tyler watched the bear and thought about that -- the store being out of bear spray. That never did add up and now they were knee-deep in a predicament. Hard to imagine the hardware store was cleaned out by the other guides. The storeowners knew hunters would be in town, and the guides that took hunters on trips always needed bear spray. The store made a point of keeping a hefty supply on hand, and if there was even a hint of it running low, they reordered. No reason to run out. But that wasn't his problem now. Now he had a woman behind him, and he was unsure where she was or how he would protect her. In front of him stood an angry and hungry bear. Night was closing in, and the path ahead of them both narrowed and steepened at a dangerous angle. What was he going to do? He didn't have many choices. He took a deep breath, and said to Ellen, "Don't move. She's going back to finish her meal. That gives us time."

"I didn't expect this," said Ellen. "What do we do now?"

"There's no way around her, and she will get very angry with us if she senses we are messing with her too much. And, there may be cubs around."

"What are you going to do?"

"We are going to back off and wait."

"We can't wait. What do you mean, wait?"

Tyler signaled to Ellen to move back with him. The bear watched them, growling again, but then went back to devouring the pile of bloody meat and bones.

Tyler pulled his knife out, checked it, and waited, and leaned against the tree.

They watched the bear and the bear watched them. Then the bear started looking in the other direction. She stood up, trying to see something further down the path, the other direction from where Tyler and Ellen were heading. Something on the other side of the bear, something

Tyler couldn't see, made the bear nervous. That was not good. The bear began to act more agitated. And Ellen, for the first time, lost her composure and screamed. The nervous bear turned her attention back to them and roared. Tyler quickly backed up, and grabbed Ellen.

He put his hand over her mouth and held her still. "What's the matter with you? Do you want to live through this? Shut up."

She struggled. "Be still and shut up." She quit fighting him and he said, "Be very quiet and I will let go of you. When I do, drop your pack." He waited a second and then added, "Are you going to do what I said?"

She nodded.

He let go of her, and took his hand off her mouth. She immediately started screaming again. Tyler caught her and again covered her mouth with his hand.

"You have gone from being a fairly reasonable woman to out of control. Now, you've started something."

The bear started swinging its head and roaring, torn between two different sources of her anger. Tyler let go of Ellen and Ellen and Tyler backed up. Ellen dropped her pack. Tyler, focused on the bear, lost track of where Ellen was. He stumbled but got up on one knee and then stood again. The bear still grew angrier and angrier. Then it decided to take its agitation out on Tyler and Ellen. Tyler backed up against a tree, ever watching the bear, knowing he couldn't look anywhere else, but the tree blocked him from running.

The bear kept coming for Tyler. Tyler dropped his pack and reached inside for his rifle, but still felt reluctant to shoot the bear. Killing it was the last resort. He tried to make himself as large and intimidating as possible, and began waving his arms. Ellen did the same, but the bear kept coming.

With no other choice, Tyler took aim with his rifle and fired -- that only enraged the bear and it sped up its attack. Tyler shot again, hitting the bear between the eyes. The animal halted in its tracks and fell in a massive, furry heap onto the forest floor.

Tyler stood very still, thinking Ellen was behind him and safe. He watched to see if the bear would move again, but she did not. On the other side of the bear, he saw a figure, a man, looking at the scene. Tyler couldn't see him clearly in the light.

"Hello!" the man said.

"Who are you, and what are you doing here?" asked Tyler

"Just a hiker, just trying one last challenge before the winter storms set in. Wasn't prepared for the bear. Didn't know what I was going to do."

Tyler walked forward, keeping his eyes on the bear and the man. Something wasn't right.

"I had bear spray, but it seemed quite inadequate considering everything," said the man as he approached the bear, looking down on it.

Tyler stood on the opposite side of the bear, eyeing both, unsure which presented greater danger.

"He's a big one, one of the biggest males I've seen. Getting ready for winter means he eats a lot of food, and this deer was a big buck."

"He is a she," said Tyler. "And I'm hopeful there aren't any cubs around. Now they're orphaned and probably won't survive."

"Ah, yes. You sound like a true woodsman, in more ways than one. You would care about the cubs."

"That's right. What is your plan, stranger?"

"Well, I guess we can all just walk around him. I need to get up the mountain and make camp for the night."

What kind of a nut is this? Something isn't right. I'm not taking my eyes off this guy, and where is Ellen?

CHAPTER 10

Tyler heard Ellen in back of him, but he didn't turn around.

"What were you thinking? Why didn't you shoot the bear?" she asked the stranger.

"I thought you were both handling it just fine. It was kind of fun to watch."

"What are you talking about?" asked Tyler. "You two know each other?"

"Meet my son," said Ellen. "He's quite talented, quite an outdoorsman. He spent quite a bit of time on this path, off and on, during these last few months, getting to know the area. And he should have shot the bear before his mother had a heart attack."

"Well, everything was going so well. It was easier than I expected, getting up here, getting the buck on the path, and attracting a bear. Seemed so wonderfully perfect, the buck was waiting for me. I had quite the outdoorsman experience. Didn't need that meat I bought. It all worked so easily that I needed to add a bit of spontaneity to the moment. It was interesting, wasn't it? Makes the story even better. I like bear melodrama."

"Well, *I don't*," said Ellen. "The bear or the cougar or the whatever wasn't supposed to show up until we were gone. This was too much."

"*What is going on?*" asked Tyler.

"We don't need to explain the whole thing to him, do we, Mother?"

"He deserves a bit of explanation." Ellen took a breath, and then said, "It took a while, but my son is now onboard to raise my granddaughter. My patience was worthwhile. I'm so happy this day has come."

"What are you talking about?" asked Tyler, keeping an eye on the man in front of him but watching Ellen emerge and stand in front of him.

"You did an excellent job, taking care of my granddaughter before she was born, and for these last four years. It's unfortunate my son didn't immediately take care of his responsibilities, but you did a good job, Tyler, until he could. But it is time. He has a wife now, and it is time. You can be assured that she will be taken care of the rest of her life. And besides that, you have another child coming. My son and Sally don't have that luxury."

"You can't be serious. You'll never get away with this. Sally is your wife?" asked Tyler, as he looked at the man.

"That's right, and she's a wonderful woman. You'll like the way she raises Clarin. And that means, of course, I'm Clarin's grandmother," said Ellen. "And, the man before you is my son, Dennis. Clarin's biological father, and Lance Goodwin's lead guitarist."

"Drop the rifle," said Dennis.

Tyler hesitated.

"Drop it now."

Tyler did as he was told and set the rifle down carefully. Tyler looked closely at Dennis. "So you are Clarin's biological father?"

"You got that right."

"Lance Goodwin's lead guitarist?"

"Yes."

Tyler remembered. It had been all over the news. *So this man was going to kidnap Clarin? This man assumed he had rights? Not going to happen.*

"Yes, we will take what is rightfully ours. And you will find the money I promised you and more back at the campsite," said Ellen.

"Move to the side, Mother" said the man.

"Why?' she asked.

He said nothing, but motioned for her to move.

"You can't be serious? You're going to shoot him? I don't believe it! Why is that necessary? Just tie him up like we planned, and we'll be out of here. Let the animals have their way with him, and if by chance he survives, and someone finds him and sets him free, so be it. We'll be long gone. Tie him up, like we planned. I don't want to watch him being shot."

"I can't do that, Mother. I can't run any risk of him surviving. He knows too much. I need to shoot him, and then let the cougars or bears take care of his body. I repeat, he knows too much. It's the only way we can be safe, Mother."

"But this isn't what we agreed on!" said Ellen.

"Mother, you have been naïve to think this would work any other way. We have to kill him and not leave it to chance. He knows too much."

"I just can't be a party to this, Dennis. There has to be some other way. He has his own child to raise now. We've got what we came for."

"We're all paying a high price for your temporary sexual indiscretions," said Tyler.

"Don't get all self-righteous with me. You have no idea what I'm about, or how hard it was to build the career I built. And you know nothing of what I have now or have the capability of building. You've lived a two-bit life, but you've taken care of my daughter, and I appreciate it. That doesn't mean you get to live. We all die at some point. This is yours."

"If you have any love for Clarin, you won't do this."

"See that, Mother? He actually loves her. Someone I didn't even know or care about. He loves her, and that's why he must die. He won't take the money and let it go. Even with another baby, he won't stop."

Ellen didn't move.

"Are you going to move, Mother? This is what needs to happen now. You need to accept that. If you want the life we so carefully planned and waited for, then you need to move. We can't change it now. Not this late in the game. You wanted me to grow up, and you like Sally. Everything is in place. We can't take chances with loose ends. I admit, I knew it had to end this way and didn't tell you. Sorry about that. But this is how it goes, and now you need to get out of the way."

"Can't you just tie him up? By the time the sheriff finds him, we'll be long gone."

"Mother, you are repeating yourself. Are you turning soft on me? Stick with what I'm telling you. Don't lose heart, now."

"What about -- ? Are you sure?"

"They're on their way. I know Sally well enough to know. We'll be together as a family, heading to South America within the hour."

Terror gripped Tyler. "You have my daughter? You have Clarin now?"

"Yes. That is what it was all about. Like I said, thank you for all your efforts. Clarin and Sally are waiting for Mother and me. Mother, move."

Ellen stood frozen. He cocked his gun.

"You would shoot me, too?"

"Move, Mother. Don't act like you didn't know it was going to end this way."

Ellen dissolved into tears.

"What is the matter, Mother? You got to know him a little bit by hiking up here? Now you want him to live? Where's that rational, scientific mind of yours?"

She stepped back, and the men could see each other clearly.

"What she said is true," said the man. "I've been slow, but now I'm here and quite willing to take charge of my responsibilities. But times have changed now. You are no longer needed. Your wife and that new baby, they have the money my mother gave you. Maybe they'll even find the rest she left at the camp. Point is, they'll do all right without you. You've served your purpose."

Tyler stalled, looking for a way out. He began to laugh. "You guys are distraught and such amateurs. You think you've covered everything, but you haven't, and now you're about to add murder to your list of crimes. Right now you haven't done anything that can't be undone. Clarin's your biological daughter, authorities might see your point in wanting her with you. Maybe even think you have the right. In time, they'll let it go. But you kill me, and they'll never stop hunting for you. We can work this out."

How? How? What was the way out?

"It's a good plan. We have a good plan. And that means we leave you here. Between this bear and your dead body, there will be plenty of bears and probably a cougar or two. It will be an untidy mess. A sorry mess. They'll never even be sure if you were murdered or attacked by an animal. I can't let you live. It will be a while before your body is discovered. That will give nature time to take its course and we will be long gone."

Tyler watched them both, knowing he had only seconds to live and was out of options, except one.

"Move farther away, Mother."

The man wanted a straight shot and Tyler wasn't going to let him have it. He lunged and grabbed an unsuspecting Ellen with the hook of his prosthesis, and pulled her in front of him, gripping her tight and shielding his hand from sight.

"Now what are you going to do?" asked Tyler. "Shoot me? Shoot both of us? You don't think you'll be found? You're mistaken. What are you going to do? Shoot your own mother?"

Dennis hesitated, and then took aim with his rifle.

"Drop it, or I'll drop you," said Tyler.

"What are you trying to do? Scare me into thinking you have a gun in that pocket?" asked Dennis.

"It's what my man Deet calls extra insurance. Better for close encounters. But if you're a real woodsmen, you oughta know that."

Dennis kept his rifle trained on them and cocked it.

Ellen broke free and Tyler fired his gun through his pocket. Dennis shot the rifle into the woods as he dropped to the ground.

"No, no!" said Ellen as she ran to her son, and kneeled there uncomprehending, watching the blood pour from his chest, "You killed him!"

She took his face in her hands. "Dennis, Dennis, speak to me." She sobbed as blood continued to flow from his body.

Tyler moved closer to her; she looked up at him and then she attacked him, screaming, and pounding his chest. Initially he let her and then held her off. She finally quit, and fell to her knees on the ground, consumed with grief, holding her face in her hands. "Get a grip," he said to Ellen. "He made his own choice. If you want to live, we've got to get out of here. It's going to get dark and cold and if the animals don't get us, hypothermia will."

"You can't just leave him here. This is my son. *My son.* You're just going to leave him here. This wasn't supposed to end this way."

"I can't? That's what you were going to do with me. You were going to kill me and leave me for the bears or the cougars. I have no way to get him out of here. But I will get you and me out. The sheriff can come for him. Or what's left of him."

Sobbing, Ellen stood and ran at Tyler, attacking him again. Tyler grabbed her, keeping her subdued, and moved her over to his pack. He tied her wrists in front, and then wound the rope several times around her middle, giving him something to hold on to from behind with his hook. He let go of her and then approached the man on the ground. Ellen stumbled toward her son and kneeled beside him, sobbing. Tyler felt his neck for a pulse again.

"He did not come back to life. He's gone." Tyler picked up the rifle, unloaded it, and stood looking at the grieving mother, bent over her son. He glanced up at the darkening sky.

"You are making jokes when I've just lost my son?" sobbed Ellen.

He ignored her statement. "Our best bet is to keep going down the path." *And meet whoever is waiting on the beach.* He went back to his pack and retrieved the light that he could wear on his head.

"Your ridiculous iridium story had me hooked for a while, but I get the larger plan. Now, everything has changed, and I want to get you and me down the mountain, and to do that we need to leave him and our packs. If I try to make camp here, we are sitting ducks for the bears, cougars, and other animals that will smell this blood. I think they are already on their way. How long will Sally wait for you to show up tonight?"

Ellen continued to sob.

"Where's my daughter?" asked Tyler.

She did not answer.

"Where's my daughter?" he asked again, putting his gun into her chin.

She looked at him defiantly and then looked away. "She's on a boat, with my son's wife, waiting for all of us."

"I get it. Leaving the country and leaving my body to be ravaged by the animals. And where is my wife?"

"I'm sure she's fine. She and Deet may have headaches, but that would be the worst of it."

Tyler, alarmed, knew he could only focus on the situation at hand. *Who knows what's going on? I've got to trust God and focus on this woman in front of me. She is the key to getting Clarin back.*

"Let's get going," said Tyler.

"You can't rescue your daughter. If my son and I don't show up on the beach, my daughter-in-law will leave and you won't ever see Clarin again."

Tyler resisted the temptation to hit her. He went over where Dennis's hat had fallen on the path and replaced his own with it.

"Get up and get going ahead of me."

"You can't expect me to go down the mountain like this. I'll fall."

"This is what you get. I'll hold onto you as best I can. I can also shoot you and leave you here with them," he said, waving at the bodies of the bear and her son. "Take it or leave it."

"Give me a minute?" she asked.

"And that's all," Tyler said.

She knelt beside her son and her grief erupted again, but after a few seconds she got up and stood quietly by her son. Tyler picked up a branch, knocked the smaller branches out of it, and with his new walking stick in his right hand and his hook on the ropes at Ellen's back, they started down the path. If she slipped, he would grab her more tightly.

Shortly they would come to the cliff, and face the treacherous trail down to the beach, and Tyler didn't know what he would do at the bottom of the cliff. He didn't know how he would rescue his daughter. But he was on the way. One step at a time. For now, they would just walk west.

CHAPTER 11

Joanne helplessly watched Rebecca, who gripped the porch railing, as Harry, the owner of the café, walked away. *What do we do now, God?* The news Harry had brought was good. Wasn't it good that he and the volunteers had found no sign of Clarin around the town or in the nearby woods? That was good, wasn't it?

Rebecca turned to Joanne. "That was good news, right?"

"Sure." *Let's not talk about how bad it could have been. Like for the men to have found Clarin hurt, or dead even, in the forest. Let's not go there, and move on.* Joanne admired Rebecca on this day. Rebecca, despite everything, remained peaceful. "Are you sure you feel okay?" asked Joanne.

"Yes, sure. I'm just not in very good shape, and I'm pregnant, but I'm peaceful. I have to trust God and I do."

"I know what we do next," said Joanne.

"What? I'm stumped. I pray, and I have no answers."

"The answer is this — we need to get you to Landing and get you checked out by the doctor there. There's a small hospital, right?"

"Yes, you're right. That's what's next. I'll get some things."

"Okay. I'm driving, get your stuff packed, but we need to leave in five minutes. We need to make sure you are okay. This is too much for a pregnant lady to deal with without medical help.

"And another thing. When all this comes to a head, and your husband and daughter are returned to you, you need to be in Landing, and ready to meet them there."

"You're saying they're going to be okay?"

"You better believe it."

"Let's pray together," said Rebecca as she turned to Joanne.

∽

Tyler and Ellen carefully forged through the hardly manageable path. One step at a time, Ellen going first, pushed and propelled by Tyler. Every once in a while, he thought about Dennis coming up this path, Dennis who was now dead, had kidnapped his daughter and intended to kill Tyler.

Every step was a challenge and a risk, however, and he needed to focus on getting himself and Ellen down the path. He couldn't save her from every branch that might be in her face, but he didn't dare go in front of her. If he weren't propelling her forward, and she decided to sit down, he would be in trouble. Whoever was looking for them to come down the cliff was looking for signs everything was okay, and that meant two people coming down. He could hear the sound of the surf growing louder; he knew they were getting close. Finally, they reached the edge of the forest, and that meant the cliff. And a little more light. They stopped and Tyler listened and looked around.

Darkness covered the ocean; all Tyler could see was the white of the waves, rolling and crashing. The sun had left a bare hint of light on the horizon, where he could see the slight bit of outline of the island that helped protect the bay. Somewhere between the island and the beach, where he couldn't see it, was a boat, a boat that held his precious daughter and person or persons who wanted to take her away from him and her mother forever.

Ellen struggled but Tyler maintained a firm hold on her. She couldn't talk, he had taped her mouth shut, but he warily looked at her and contemplated how to get to the beach, how to rescue his daughter, and how to stay alive. He would take as long as he needed, under the shadow of the trees, to think the situation through. As long as he and Ellen were hidden, they were safe. And his daughter was safe.

∼

Deet and the small boat bounced through the swells, steadily making progress toward the rocky island and the small bay that it protected. He couldn't go any faster, for fear that the sound would alert those he wanted to surprise. Finally, he approached the island. As he came around the side of the island, he slowed the motor, and the water calmed. He could see the boat anchored ahead of him between the island and the mainland.

He hovered in the water, thinking it through. Clarin was likely on the boat with Sally, waiting for whoever to come down the cliff? It had to be Ellen and the only other person who had an interest in kidnapping the little girl, Clarin's biological father, Sally's husband and Ellen's son? Would they have killed Tyler? Dear Lord, he hoped not, but given the situation that had to have been the plan. Why go through the ruse to lure him off alone, if it wasn't. Nobody would know what happened to him, and it would allow for a good getaway. But Tyler was no fool. If Deet had to bet on anybody surviving in that forest, he would bet on Tyler. He would bet on Tyler coming down that cliff, wanting to get to that boat and rescue his daughter. Either way, Deet knew he needed to get to that boat, unseen, and take out whoever was on the boat and get the little girl.

The sound of the waves on the shore of the mainland would help muffle some engine noise. The darkness of the night helped, but the biggest advantage was that whoever was on the boat was likely watching the shore, waiting for Ellen and her son They wouldn't be looking toward the island.

Deet kept the motor on low, and maneuvered his small craft between the island and the larger boat. He knew currents, wind, and boats, and he knew how to evaluate each and get his boat positioned just perfectly. When he was satisfied, he turned off the motor.

The little boat bobbed in the water, a light spray hitting him in the face every few seconds. He kept his eyes on his goal. He did not feel the water or the wind, or get sick from the motion of the boat. Ever so slowly the little boat moved closer to the larger one.

He could see a light on in the cabin. He saw one figure move on the deck.

Then his boat drifted too far to the south. He used one of the paddles to steer the boat back on course, closer and closer to the goal.

∽

"I can and will kill you at any time, do you understand that?" said Tyler

She nodded.

"I need to know what kind of signal you and Dennis had planned at this point. You had to have a signal to let them know you were coming down this hill. That I was dead, and everything was a go. I want to know that signal." She looked at him with frightened eyes.

He shook her. "Do you want to live?"

She nodded. He ripped the tape from her mouth. She winced in pain.

"It's a light. I know that. Tell me what the signal is. *Now*," said Tyler.

"It's just three short flashes, and then wait for the same as a response. Then we were to know it is safe to come down; we would use the boat that Dennis left there, and join them as soon as we could."

"What kind of light?"

"It's in my jacket pocket."

He reached in and found the light. Looking at it, he practiced using it.

"If this doesn't work, if you've told me wrong, you're dead."

Ellen nodded and said, "I told you the truth. As soon as you flash three short ones, she'll reply, and then it's all right for us to continue on."

She was his only hope. If the people on the boat knew that Dennis was dead and if Ellen was dead, he would lose. They started down the hill, sliding, holding onto whatever they could. Tyler stopped their descent and sent the signal, and the return signal came promptly from the boat. With any luck at all, Sally would remember the rest of the plan, and not focus on watching them come down the cliff. She would, as agreed upon, start up the engine and prepare the boat for the long trip south.

"I'm going to leave the tape off your mouth, in case Ellen wants to talk to you. Your only chance is you have both of us on that boat. Do you see that?"

Tyler didn't know who was on the boat, besides Sally and Clarin, and he didn't bother asking Ellen.

"You're my ticket to getting on that boat. Sally is no doubt looking to see that there are two of us coming down this god-forsaken cliff. I have to keep you alive." Ellen nodded in agreement and said, "I understand."

Tyler knew he couldn't trust her. At any moment, Sally and Ellen, or either one of them, would easily get rid of him.

"I'm going to take us down the side, close to the trees, so they can't see us very well. I'm still going to leave the tape off."

Ellen nodded yes.

At Tyler's direction, Ellen sat on the ground and inched herself down through the steep incline. When her right foot flailed in midair, she gasped and reached behind her for something to hold onto. Grabbing Tyler's foot, she clung on for dear life.

"It's a drop off," said Tyler. "We've got to go sidewise, into the trees, and go down through the trees. We can't go any farther this way."

"I don't think I can move," said Ellen. "I can't let go of your ankle, and I can't grab anything else."

She couldn't see what Tyler was doing, but she felt his hand on her upper arm pulling her up, and then she felt his other arm, with the hook, circle her body. He dragged both of them along the steep embankment, slowly, one inch at a time, until she felt grass on her face. Relieved, she wanted to stop, but he wouldn't let her. Her mouth tasted foul, like rocks and blood. Finally, when she reached out for what felt like the one hundredth time, she touched what she knew was a rock. She curled up next to the rock, exhausted, not caring what Tyler was doing.

"Keep going until we get to a tree," he said.

"I'm not moving. I can't see. I can't move any farther."

"Keep moving! You don't have far to go. That rock could let go at any time."

Ellen knew Tyler was close, but was he close enough to catch her if she started tumbling down the incline? He wasn't touching her, no doubt trying to stay safe himself. She could hear his breath, as labored as her own.

"Get going, I can see the tree line not far ahead," he said.

Ellen was afraid to look up, afraid to do anything, but inch herself along in the rocks that scraped her face.

She moved forward, hearing the small rocks that she dislodged tumbling down, and down and down.

She moved herself across the steep incline, crawling like a lizard.

Then she touched something different. She stopped and felt with her fingers. A tree. With a big trunk.

"That's right. It's big enough to hold you," said Tyler. "Get yourself wrapped around it."

She did as she was told, glad to stop, glad to feel the security of the tree trunk. After a while, she opened her eyes and was aware of Tyler beside her. She saw more trees ahead of them. So they had almost made it to the tree line.

"When we get to the trees, it will be easier, but not a whole lot," he said.

She nodded, and listened to the crashing surf. In the darkness, she could see the white foam of the waves, waves that weren't so big because of the protection of the island and the bay. And down there, directly below them, was the boat that she and Dennis had planned to take out to the larger boat where Ellen and Clarin now awaited them.

And now, here she was, everything had changed. Dennis was dead and she was dependent on Tyler for her life -- to get her down this cliff in the dark, onto the boat, out to the bigger boat, where Clarin, precious Clarin awaited her.

"It would help, of course, if we could use the light I brought, but I can't take that chance. We'll make it, but we're going to make good use of this rope and my hook."

He tied a knot in the rope and put it over her head and shoulders.

"Do the very best you can to get the rest of the way down, but if you slip and fall, this will catch you."

"What's going to keep you from being pulled down with me?" she asked.

"My hook," he said holding up his left arm. "I can sink into a tree, or softer ground."

Ellen looked at it in horror, knowing he could also do a lot of damage to her body with it. "Give me a minute," she said.

Ellen had not been much of a praying woman, but she then spoke to God, silently praying, *if you are there, please let me live through this. Please.* She looked out at the steep incline, the dark shadows of the trees, and wondered if she heard God speak to her, would she recognize it. She had to live. She had to live out the plan that she and Dennis had striven toward. He would want her to carry on. Sally and Clarin depended on her now. She had to live and she had to carry on their plans. Precious Clarin, who now slept peacefully in the boat anchored out in the bay. Precious Clarin depended on her.

She started slowly down, aware that her feet and ankles were vulnerable, aware of Tyler right above her, moving slowly. Only vaguely aware that she was getting very dirty, and who really cared? The main thing was to get on that boat, get on their way to their new life, and get rid of Tyler at the appropriate time.

"Okay. We're making it. I've got you. I'm not going to take these ropes off you. Remember what I said. Your best chance to survive is help me get on that boat. I could care less if you get away. But you ruin my chance to do that, I'll kill you."

She kept going, knowing Dennis would want her to succeed in this.

Tyler spoke again, "Do you understand?"
She nodded, and said "Yes." *I hate him. Disgusting human being.*

~

They kept going down the hill, following the tree line, Tyler only using the flashlight for brief moments when he needed help. There were rough steps going all the way to the beach, but he avoided those, knowing they could be seen with infrared glasses. He needed for whoever was on that boat to not know that Dennis was not coming down the hill. And, he did not know how secure the steps were. One dislodged step could mean disaster.

As they got closer to the beach, Ellen started to stand up too soon, and she lost her balance and fell. Tyler off-balance, fell on top of her. They both rolled the rest of the way down, and they stopped when they reached the beach. The soft sand was a relief. Tyler felt every bone in his body and could hardly breathe. Did he break anything? Ellen was sitting up, he had to get up, no matter how he felt or what he had broken. They both sat still, struggling to breathe, and unable to talk.

Finally, Tyler asked, "Where's the boat you're supposed to have on the beach?"

"Dennis said he would leave it close by, near the cliff."

They both stood and slowly walked through the sand dunes toward the water. They found the boat before they had gone far. Each of them picked up a side, and started pulling it toward the waves. When they reached the water, they waded through it until it was knee deep.

"Put the boat down," said Tyler. He took the duct tape out of his pocket, ripped off a section, and told her to put it over her mouth.

Ellen hesitated.

"Do it, or you're toast."

She put the tape over her mouth and pressed it down.

"Press harder," said Tyler.

Ellen did as she was told.

"Climb into the boat," he said. It was chancy to have her wrists tied together in front of her, but she had to be able to climb into this boat and climb up the ladder of the bigger boat.

Then Tyler rolled himself into the boat and sat down in the back, where he pushed the motor back and tried to start the engine.

It wouldn't start. He tried again. On the third try it started. He let the motor warm up as the little boat rocked gently among the swells. His eyes scanned the dark water between them and the island. He could see a faint light out there, very faint.

"I see the light on the boat," said Tyler.

Ellen leaned forward, looking. She nodded. Tyler started toward the larger boat, gently bucking the swells.

He wished the little engine wasn't so loud, but he couldn't do anything about it.

Now, for the first time, he thought about getting on the boat, and successfully staying alive, rescuing his daughter. What he knew for certain was that he had to go first, or he was doomed. He thought of throwing Ellen overboard once he was next to the bigger boat, but he wasn't a cold-blooded killer like Ellen's son. He wouldn't do that unless she made it so he had to.

Tyler kept Dennis's hat low over his face and angled the boat toward the larger boat. Ellen sat in front of him, facing him.

They got past the swells and waves, and steadily moved toward the larger boat. He wasn't afraid of someone flashing a light on them. He was wearing Dennis's hat, he was following the prearranged plan, and putting a light on them would only bring attention to anyone else in the area. He slowed the motor and moved up next to the larger boat, quickly tied on and then started up the ladder before Sally could be alerted. Ellen knew that if she got that tape off and yelled something, he would kill her, and he counted on that knowledge keeping her in line. Tyler quickly pulled himself up the ladder and swung onto the deck just as Sally came out of the cabin. "Dennis!" She moved toward him and then stopped.

"You! Where did you come from?"

"Where's my daughter?"

"She's my daughter now, and she's sleeping. She'll be fine."

"She isn't your daughter, and you and your mother aren't going anywhere with her."

Sally's face went gray. "Where's Dennis?"

"He's dead. And you will be too if you don't cooperate with me."

Tyler watched her face. She seemed to not comprehend what he said. She leaned over the side of the boat and saw her mother-in-law struggling with the duct tape on her mouth. Watching Tyler and Ellen at the same time, Sally screamed, "Where's Dennis?"

Ellen finally ripped the tape from her mouth.

"Sally, Dennis is dead. I'm coming aboard. Tyler has a gun, be careful!"

Tyler, anxious to find his daughter, knew he could not leave the two women alone. He watched Ellen start up the ladder. Right when she was within reach, she slipped and screamed, dangling on the ladder.

Tyler moved closer and bent over to grab her. He got his hand around her wrist, ready to bring her in when he saw Sally coming at him with a hammer.

"I'll drop her!" said Tyler.

Sally hesitated just a second and then kept coming. Tyler let go of Ellen and turned to Sally blocking her assault and then pushing her back against the cabin. She gasped for breath. He kept her pinned against the cabin and yelled into her face, "What kind of a crazy person are you?"

"You killed my Dennis and you have ruined our plans. I want to kill you!"

She struggled again and Tyler could tell by her eyes that Ellen was behind him.

Tyler slammed Sally against the cabin and she fell unconscious to the floor. He quickly turned around and stopped Ellen's screaming assault. In her tied together hands, she held a knife. Tyler threw her against the cabin, and then she also sunk to the floor, unconscious.

He stepped down into the cabin and listened carefully. He heard nothing. Was it possible, even likely, that the two women and Dennis were going to pull this off on their own? That the only other person on board was his daughter?

Quietly and carefully walking down the corridor, Tyler listened at the first door and then quietly opened it. Nothing.

He went to the next door and listened. Nothing. He opened the door and heard a rustle. He turned on the light, and there lay Clarin on the bed covered with a blanket.

"Oh, my precious daughter. Thank you, God." Tyler knelt down beside her and buried his face in her hair.

"Daddy? Daddy? Are you crying?"

He looked at her and smiled, stroking her hair. "Yeah, baby girl, I guess I was."

"Where's Mommy? Where am I? I want to go home."

"Me, too, baby girl. Me too. We're on a boat, but I'll get us home soon."

Clarin put her arms round Tyler. "I love you, Daddy."

Once again, Tyler buried his face in her hair and wept. "Thank you, God."

Back on deck, Tyler looked at the lumps that were Ellen and Sally. They would stay out for a while longer, he hoped. He needed to get the boat started and into Landing, and turn these women over to the sheriff. He saw something out in the water. He could tell it was a person, a man, another accomplice maybe? He went to the side of the boat and prepared for a fight, but to his relief, he saw Deet pulling alongside.

"What are you doing out here in the middle of nowhere?" asked Tyler.

"I heard you had some trouble and thought I might come watch you handle it."

"That's right I did, more than I bargained for. These two women and the man that I have left dead on the path, were trying to kidnap my daughter and I have handled it, but I would like some help getting these two women and my daughter back to shore. It's a lot for one person to keep an eye on all at once. You are supposed to be the sheriff, and this seems like a situation that involves the authorities."

He took a deep breath. His heart had been pumping on adrenal and its beat finally began to slow. "So what have you been doing? How is my wife?"

"She's fine. When she and Joanne and I figured out what was going on, I left them in Crystal and got a boat. Thought you might need some help. Evidently not. You've got the thing under control."

"So you're all the help I get with a kidnapping? And a planned murder? Mine, by the way. Let's get that boat tied up and you on board. Let the other one go. No reason to try to tow two boats."

He took the line Deet threw him and tied it on the stern of the larger boat.

Deet started to climb onto the larger boat. "Big traffic pile up south of Landing. All the law enforcement is busy there. I'm all you got today. By the way, Joanne and I weren't that lucky. That Sally can deliver a wallop, I'll say. So we were a little delayed, figuring the whole thing out. I'll tell you about it later."

Tyler noticed a fast change in Deet's expression as he stepped onto the boat. Tyler started to turn around, but not in time to dodge Ellen's attack. She wielded an ax from the boat. It was too heavy for her to lift, but she hit Tyler's leg with it and dropped him to his knees. The momentum threw her off balance. She lost her grip on the ax, careened against the rail, and then fell overboard, screaming. Tyler heard a hard thud that put a sudden stop to Ellen's screams. He peered over the side and saw where she'd landed with her lower half in the water, and upper half in the smaller boat. He was pretty sure the thud he'd heard was her head making contact with the boat's bench seat.

Tyler grasped the rail, consumed with pain. He pulled himself up but was unable to walk. Deet hurried back into the smaller boat and pulled Ellen over its side.

The pain in Tyler's right leg kept him bent over the rail while Deet moved Ellen's limp body. She looked small and harmless.

"Is she still alive?" asked Tyler.

Deet put his hand on her neck. "I can't tell. I'm going to get us out of here before the storm comes in. That's my priority."

Tyler sunk down on the deck, unable to help himself any more.

Oh, Lord. Are you there? Are you there?

A darkness folded in on him.

Deet pulled the outboard motor up out of the water, made sure it was secure. He looked at the unconscious Ellen lying in the bottom of the small boat. This was all he could do here. He climbed up the ladder onto the deck and went to the stern to make sure it was securely tied. He watched the little boat bobbing up and down, the limp body reminded him of the reality of the night. *Maybe it's safer that way. If she comes back to life, she can't attack Tyler or me.* He looked at Tyler passed out, but breathing. Likely from pain, no blood running from his body. *I'll leave him there.* Sally was still alive but in a crumpled heap on the deck; he was wary of her. He knew firsthand what she was capable of. He wasn't going to take any chances so he took the rope off the deck and quickly tied her up. *Now, where is that Clarin?*

He went down below, peered into several cabins, and then found Clarin under a blanket. He pulled back the blanket and looked into her wide eyes.

"Mr. Deet!" she said as she threw her arms around his neck. "My daddy said to stay here no matter what I heard, but I was scared!"

"You did good, honey. You did what your daddy said, and I want you to stay right here, until I get this boat docked in Landing."

"Is my daddy okay?"

"He's going to be fine. He's taking a nap. You stay here, and stay warm, and I'll come get you when we've docked the boat. Promise me you'll stay right here?"

"I promise. You're sure my daddy's okay?"

"I'm sure," he said with all the assurance he could muster.

"Where's my mommy?"

"You're going to see your mommy when we get back to shore. She's okay. You stay here, like you promised, and before you know it we'll be back on shore, and everything is going to be okay."

Deet hesitated and then bent over and kissed her on the top of her head. She smiled and lay back on the bunk. He covered her up, patted her head, and went back up the ladder to the deck.

Deet started the boat, checked on all passengers, who were still all lying unconscious, as he had left them, and then put the boat in gear and started for Landing. Steady as she goes, not fast, not slow, but in the dark, using the radar, he headed out of the bay, and past the island. As he turned south, he slowed the boat down and went on the marine radio to the sheriff's office in Landing.

"This is Deputy Sheriff Deet. I'm coming into the west dock with four passengers. One is a child. I'm thirty minutes away -- and they all are in immediate need of medical assistance. Two of them need to be arrested."

"And why didn't you do that yourself, Deputy Sheriff Deet?"

"*I'm busy.*"

The rain started. Deet took the boats out into the rougher water, and headed for Landing.

∼

"I feel fine. Nobody seems worried about anything. I want to go down to the marina and see my husband and daughter." Rebecca looked defiantly at Joanne, and Joanne, considering everything that had happened, wanted no part of this decision.

"Let's wait here until the doctor returns. You might rest, there's plenty of time to get down there."

Rebecca didn't realize how tired and stressed she looked. Understandably, she wanted to see her little daughter and her husband, but she didn't look good.

The doctor came in, all smiles, looking at the information on the computer he carried.

"You are doing well," said the doctor. "I am pleased, and the baby looks good."

Rebecca closed her eyes and started to weep. Silent big tears rolled down her face.

"Thank you, God. And now, doctor, can I get dressed and get down to the marina to meet my husband and daughter. I presume that's okay?" She started to sit up.

"Not so fast, young lady," the doctor said as he gently pressed her back onto the bed.

"What on earth do you mean? We are through. I want to go down to the marina. You said yourself I was okay. Everything looks good."

"That's right," said the doctor. "Everything on the charts looks good, all the tests look good. But, I am a doctor, I don't rely solely on tests and charts, and I say you are staying right here in this hospital overnight, so we can keep an eye on you."

Rebecca sighed deeply and turned away from the doctor. "You are so irritating," she said.

"I hear that a lot from my wife," he said, smiling. "Do as I say. Your family will be coming here for their own checkups. Don't argue with me or cross me. Don't try to be a hero." He bent down and looked at her eye-to-eye.

"Did you hear me?"

She nodded.

"Are you going to do what I say?"

She nodded again.

He looked at Joanne. "And don't you try to do anything similar to what they do in the movies, like try to help her escape from the hospital. Got that?"

"Oh, yessir. You'll have no problems with me. I'll tie her to the bed if necessary."

∾

Deet struggled to keep the boat on course; it jumped and bobbed through the swells, the spray attacking the glass, over and over again. He finally could see the light of the end of the breakwater. Steady, steady he went as he approached the Landing marina. Once past the breakwater, the waters calmed some, but he kept going. The relentless storm was on his back. He could see the swinging light on the dock, and he knew that was the sheriff signaling him to come on in. *Come here, and we'll get your boat docked.* The waters churned and the boat bucked -- Deet slowed the boat, and had a hard time maintaining control. This wasn't going to be easy. He aimed for the dock and hoped for the best. He could see the men, several of them, waiting on the dock to help.

Deet rammed the dock on the front right side of the boat. He cut the engine and threw the lines over to the waiting men. They pulled the boat in and tied her down. Deet pushed the ladder down, and his boss, the sheriff, stepped aboard.

"Deputy Sheriff Deet, I understand you have passengers."

"That's right. The most important being a very special little girl down in the cabin. That's her daddy, right there, a little worse for wear, and these two women," he pointed to Sally and then took the sheriff to the stern, where he pointed out the towed dingy and the body in it, "these two women are in a heap of trouble."

"Why don't you go stay with Clarin, since she knows you, and give us a few minutes to get these people taken care of. Probably upset her to see all of this."

"Yessir," said Deet, as he started toward the cabin door.

"And Deet," said the sheriff.

Deet turned around.

"Deet, I'm awfully proud of you."

Deet went back down the steps and down the hallway to Clarin. He found her just where he had left her. Her frightened face peered from the blanket.

"Deet, the boat banged loud!"

He knelt beside her and smiled. "I know. Scary, wasn't it? But the boat is docked, we are all safe now, and in a few minutes you can see your dad, and then we'll go see your mom."

"Is my daddy okay? Is he still sleeping?"

"He's going to have a few aches and pains, but the doctor will fix him up."

Tyler, meanwhile, thought he was answering the EMT's questions, but he wasn't sure. What he knew was that he was glad to see them, and whatever they gave him for the pain in his leg, he was glad of it. He could stand it a little while longer, until it took effect. But at least they had given him something. The two young men loaded him onto a stretcher, and then carried him to the side of the boat, where he was lowered to two other men, and they carried him down the dock.

They opened the doors to the ambulance, and lifted him and the stretcher into the back and strapped down the stretcher. Before they shut the door, Tyler said, "I need to see my daughter, *now*."

"Sir, the deputy is bringing her."

"I want her in this ambulance with me, and we'll wait for that to happen."

"Sir, they are coming, we really need to get you to the hospital. Your wife is waiting for you at the hospital. Your daughter will follow in the second ambulance."

"*No*. We aren't leaving until my daughter shows up, dammit."

Tyler stared at the ceiling and waited, refusing to do anything else. The rain pelted on top of the ambulance.

The sheriff stepped into the ambulance and said to Tyler, "Can you answer some questions before they take you to the hospital?"

"Probably not," said Tyler, "but after I get my hands on my daughter, and see my wife, then I'll answer anything you want."

"Fair enough," said the sheriff. The doors opened again, and Deet stepped in with Clarin wrapped in his arms.

"Daddy, Daddy!" said the little girl as she strained to get away from Deet and throw herself on Tyler.

"Daddy, I was scared, and I didn't know where you were. You rescued me!"

"Yes, I did, and then Deet rescued both of us." He held her close, for a long time, not saying anything. The sheriff and the EMTs waited until he finally let go of her.

"Daddy, are we going to ride in an ambulance? I've never done that before."

"That's what we're going to do. Let's go see the doctors and your mommy."

∼

Joanne sat anxiously beside Rebecca, not knowing what to do. The doctor opened the door slightly and motioned for Joanne to join him in the hall.

She did as he asked, and he said, "They made it safely to the marina here in Landing. Rebecca's husband will need some medical attention. We'll bring them to Rebecca's room for a visit as soon as possible."

"What do you want me to do?"

"We've got another emergency and we're focused on that. Your job is to keep Rebecca here, and calm, until her family shows up. No moving around, or trying to find them."

"I can do that."

"Good. We're a small hospital. It's all hands-on deck. I'll be back."

Joanne returned to the room. Rebecca's eyes were closed, but they popped open as soon as Joanne sat down.

"What did the doctor say?" asked Rebecca.

"He said your husband and daughter are on their way. They will come to your room, when it is appropriate, and you are to stay put."

Rebecca closed her eyes, "I can actually do that. No need to think I'm going to get up and run around. Are they okay? Please tell me they are okay?"

"Looks like Clarin is in good shape. Tyler is a bit beat up, but nothing life-threatening. They will get a good going-over here in the hospital."

Rebecca's eyes popped open again. "Do you have a mirror?" she asked Joanne.

Joanne found a small one in her purse and handed it to Rebecca, who looked at herself and then said, "I look white and wasted. It will worry Clarin. Not Tyler, but Clarin."

Joanne found a lipstick in her purse and opened it. "Do you like this color? Will Clarin like it?"

"Love it. Better than ghostly white. Thanks. Thanks for being such a good friend."

Right. *If you only knew how my meddlesome ways helped bring this on.*

Rebecca sank back against her pillow and Joanne, convinced she was sleeping, went to the window. She looked out at the wet dark night, the parking lot below her, and thought of the mess which she, herself, had helped create.

And what about my own daughter? She's so wonderful, so beautiful, but what have I done to her, by always being such a guiding force in her life, and never giving her much of a chance to make her own decisions and fail? What kind of boys would Jasmine be interested in dating in college? What principles did Jasmine grow up with, other than the importance of being saved and doing well in school?

The glory of this whole experience was now severely tarnished. I will have to figure out my part of the story and make amends. And I will do the same with my marriage. Instead of letting Larry take all the blame, I will look at it all more honestly. I can do that for Jasmine. I can do that for the God I love, who surely wants me, Larry, and Jasmine to have better lives, to be a credit to God, rather than just blithely go on, as if it doesn't matter. It matters.

She turned and looked at Rebecca. Sleeping, but fatigue showing on her face. Rebecca wasn't going anywhere. *I will leave now, I'm not ready to face Tyler. They will be here soon and they will need their privacy.*

Joanne looked down into the parking lot and saw the ambulances arriving. *Yes, it's okay to leave Rebecca now.*

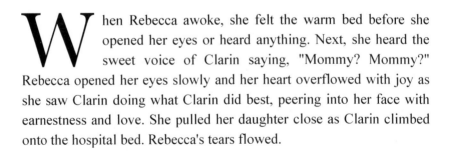

When Rebecca awoke, she felt the warm bed before she opened her eyes or heard anything. Next, she heard the sweet voice of Clarin saying, "Mommy? Mommy?" Rebecca opened her eyes slowly and her heart overflowed with joy as she saw Clarin doing what Clarin did best, peering into her face with earnestness and love. She pulled her daughter close as Clarin climbed onto the hospital bed. Rebecca's tears flowed.

"There they are, my two beautiful women," said that strong male voice that Rebecca loved to hear.

She opened her eyes to see Tyler standing in front of her. She smiled as he leaned over to kiss her.

"What's with the cane?" she asked. "I love my one-armed husband, but I don't know about three legs, that's a bit strange." She smiled at him, deliriously happy.

"Yeah, well, I'll be awhile getting back to two legs. I understand you and the little one are okay. That we're all okay, but they'll keep us here for the night. Just to be sure."

"Then let's go home, and be very thankful to God for so very much."

"I agree with that. Let's go home and be so very thankful. God has blessed us. And let's not forget Deet among those we are grateful for. I think the sheriff wants to talk to me a bit more. I'll be back." He leaned over to kiss her and Clarin again and went into the hallway.

∽

"He's dead, sheriff. He was intending to kill me, but it's him laying up there. I imagine the bears and a cat or two have had their way with him by now."

The sheriff closed his notebook. "You're fortunate to be alive. And you're lucky you have bones of steel. The legal system will have its way with the two women. I'll know where to find you when you're needed."

"They evidently gave my wife no drugs, she was already tired and sleepy, but they did give Clarin something. I'm glad we are all going to spend the time in the hospital. I have faith, however, that we'll leave in the morning with a clean bill of health for all."

"We'll be back to the scene in the morning. Might be time to tell the public we need some more deputies. Of course, Deet does the work of three."

Tyler smiled. "That's true. Do you think that massive car wreck south of town, taking up all your time, do you think that was part of this scheme? Those twisted people were not afraid to do anything, it seems."

"Everything is under investigation. I've got everything I need for now. Get some sleep. If that's possible."

"I am thankful. My God, these are twisted people. When I married Rebecca, that little girl became mine and that was all there was to it. All Rebecca said at the time was an indiscretion involving drugs and a concert. I didn't need to know anymore. Clarin was and is mine."

"Like you said, they are twisted. They are both going away for a long time. Might be that Dennis got the better deal."

∼

Tyler studied the magazine lying on the counter, and then set the temperature on the stove.

"Can I help?" asked Rebecca.

"No. Absolutely not. This recipe is from one of your magazines, and I aim to create a treat for my women. This is my job and I'm doing it. Poached eggs in the oven. Prepare to be amazed. Just please tell me where to find a muffin tin." He turned to look at his wife and daughter at the table.

Rebecca laughed and pointed at a lower cabinet. "It's down there with the *iridium*."

"That wasn't funny," said Tyler as he found it and then filled each cup with water.

"That is a creative thing you're doing," Rebecca said. "I'm impressed."

"Yes, my women deserve my very best." He turned to watch them.

Clarin had filled ¾ of the table with her miniature train set, and Rebecca sat beside her drinking coffee.

"Mama, I want to put horses on the train. Daddy's horses."

Rebecca looked through the small box on the table, full of extra train cars, animals, people, and she found two grown horses and a foal. Clarin flashed a smile and put the horses in the open train car.

"I love you," Tyler said quietly.

Rebecca and Clarin looked up at him. Did they see his tears? Clarin went back to playing with the train, but Rebecca stood up and came to him and put her arms around him.

After breakfast, Tyler had a tough time keeping his eyes off his wife and daughter but he knew it was time to go check on his horses, so he broke away from them to go to his barn. As he was walking down the street, Joanne approached him. He did not stop and so she hurried to keep up with him.

"I want to apologize to you for getting involved in your business, and the awfulness of it all, and I ask you for forgiveness."

Tyler stopped and looked at her.

"You were way out of line. New here. Not your business anyway. These women, they took you in, and respected you, and you abused that. These women, including my wife, are not as worldly as you, and they trusted you and looked up to you, and you took advantage of that. You manipulated them and me. As for me, I'm responsible for my decisions, and I made a bad one. I take responsibility for my decisions. In some ways horses are smarter than humans. They can sense something wrong in a person. What you did, while not overtly wrong, was still wrong. In subtle ways, you undermined my chance, my wife's chance, to wait, evaluate our situation and the people. We need to develop our own discernment muscle. Trust our own guts. Maybe you would call that the Holy Spirit. I don't know."

"Will you forgive me?"

"I'm not looking to forgive you right away. You are representing a type of Christianity that I don't like. Preach a good sermon about salvation, but don't walk a walk that I respect. You thought you knew what was best, and you were pretty prideful about it."

"I'm so upset. I meant well."

"It's still about you, isn't it? I don't think you get it that whether or not you are upset is not the main issue here. I don't care if you are upset or not. You are more upset that someone, me for instance, would think less of you than you are of what you did."

"When will you forgive me?"

Tyler shook his head. She wasn't going to get it.

"When is none of your business. But for your own sake, I hope you can come to terms with the reality of what happened and your part in it. Maybe we can have a conversation then."

"I, as a Christian woman, have greatly wounded you, and I must have your forgiveness."

"Shut up with the Christianese. Just shut up with that talk. It doesn't even make any sense to me. I have good friends here. Pastor Andy is a longtime friend. I have respect for him and the church he's trying to build. We have mutual friends, Collin and Julie, who will be here for Thanksgiving. But while I have great respect for Andy and this church he is building, I have no respect for you, or Christians like you, who are so self-righteous, think they know better than anyone else, and see that as an excuse to meddle, to try and play God when you don't know what needs to be done in someone else's life."

"I know. I deserve that."

"Oh, I don't think you do. Not at all. You are just super concerned with how you look, that you haven't "glorified God," and I don't think you have any idea about what exactly happened. What I know is this. I, and my wife, we will learn from this, and we will take our time to do it. I suggest you do the same. But you do whatever."

"I think you're right. I really haven't come to grips with what happened and my part."

"You're probably saying that just to get me to like you, to forgive you, because it's all so painful. You would be right. It's painful, and scary, and I tell you this, out there in the forest, facing an angry bear and two crazy people, not knowing whether or not I would see my daughter and wife again, that was pretty scary."

Joanne's eyes widened at his description and she put her hand to her mouth and gasped. It was the first show of empathy he'd seen from the woman.

Tyler sighed. "I'll probably forgive you before this day is over. Won't do me any good to haul the whole thing around, but that doesn't mean I trust you or want my family to spend any time with you. But I'll be polite, because of Andy."

"I so much wanted to help Andy build this church," said Joanne. "I meant well. I guess I said that before. I don't know what to say."

"If my friends Collin and Julie show up, I'll be interested in having dinner with them, in the new house church, and if you're there, that's okay. But right now, the issues that Andy and I talk about -- the necessity for belonging to a church, well you've proven my point. My friend Deet and some others, they have earned my trust. And sometimes he makes a strong opinion, but he leaves it at that. He always makes it clear he trusts my decisions. And his connection with God is pretty damn strong. I think your salvation message is pretty worthless, considering your walk and your talk. I'd done a lot better to trust God and myself, rather than listen to you."

Joanne felt the blood drain out of her face. She didn't know what to say or do.

"I wish you well," said Tyler, and he kept walking. Joanne stopped and watched him. She felt her face burning. She turned and put one foot in front of another, all the way back to Andy's house. She waved at people as they waved at her, but deep inside she wanted to get inside the house and shut the door.

I need to talk to Andy.

CHAPTER 12

"Heh, Jas, it's Dad. I've got a surprise for you. Let's go to lunch tomorrow. Are you free?"

Jasmine breathed in and out. *So this is how it happens. You figure out how your parents screwed you, you finally get out from under them, and you figure it out, with the help of your friends, and you stand firm, and then the miracle happens, and your dad calls. Amazing.*

"Yeah, Dad, I'm free. What time?"

"I'll be there at about 11:30. You'll like this lunch. I'll see you then."

After Jasmine finished the phone call, she lay back on her bed, feeling the joy of the success.

"You really do look like the cat who swallowed the mouse, or whatever that saying is," said her roommate.

"I have no doubt. Some things take a long time coming, but they do arrive. My dad is coming tomorrow, and after all we've been through for the past year, he is, amazingly, coming to see me. We will have a good talk. I, at last, have some power."

"Great for you. Just great. Now maybe you can help me?"

"Oh, really, like you have any problems, Miss Perfect."

"Come on, don't do that. I've got an exam this morning in Business Law101, and I need some help. Like someone to quiz me."

"All right. I have between 9 and 10 open. You want to meet in the library?"

Her roommate nodded just as her phone rang. She answered and Jasmine listened; how could she not?

"Mom, how could you say that? How can you take that from him?"

Jasmine continued to listen to one side of the conversation. How strange the transition most of them had made, from their cushy lives at home, wherever that was, where they had nice clothes enough for three people, theater tickets, unlimited supply of gas in the tank, courtesy of parents, of course, to here, where they all lived simply, shared ideas, studied together, and learned from each other. Learning to apply themselves without mother's prompting, and how to separate themselves from their parents. Jasmine felt lucky, her own transition was going well, as evidenced by the phone message from her dad.

Her mother, now that would take some extra time, some extra thought. Joanne looked so good on the surface, did so many good things, it was hard to pinpoint what was wrong there, but Jasmine knew one thing, she was tired of the subtle ways her mom wanted to steer her life.

Jasmine liked being away from her, and hearing her own thoughts and making her own decisions. Even the ability to get rid of the comforter her mother had bought for her and get her own, green instead of blue, all of that empowered Jasmine.

Her dad, now he was a piece of work, but in some ways easier to handle than her mother. He obviously screwed up, made no pretense of being perfect, and found no need to micromanage Jasmine's life. And proof of her own power and her dad's better attitude toward life, he was the one who called and wanted to have lunch with her and talk. Right there, clear as day, he and Jasmine would be open, frank, honest, and clean up their issues. One parent at a time. The easy one first.

As Jasmine listened to her roommate go on and on with her own mother, she congratulated herself with the ease with which she and her father had made this transition. Not everyone was as fortunate. They were people, all of them flawed, but people of some extraordinary abilities, and she was pleased with that.

Jasmine got dressed and left her dorm room with her roommate and her mother still going strong on their family issues.

On the way to the downstairs cafeteria, feeling the success of the day, Jasmine passed Carl at the coffee machine. So cute, so tall, and such a wonderful smile.

"Heh, Jasmine. Are you going out to dinner and on the midnight hike with us tomorrow?"

He was so good-looking, and he was talking to her, but she also knew the hike had a price — fifty dollars to pay for the meal catered at the mountain.

"I'm not sure." That was hard. She would have loved to look right into his smiling brown eyes and say yes. But it wasn't right yet. She had no transportation from the downtown library, where she needed to study, and didn't know anybody well enough to ask for a ride. The whole thing was a bit expensive all the way around.

~

"Hi, Dad!" said Jasmine with all the enthusiasm and love she could gather. This was important, this was a big step forward for her family and she was grateful and wanted to be encouraging. The new openness and transparency, that was beginning. Right now. *And I started it.*

He gave her a big hug and then she inserted herself into the big booth. Way too big for both of them, but it afforded privacy.

"How's your mother doing? I haven't heard much from her since she went to Washington State," her dad said after he had ordered.

"I haven't heard too much either. Just brief postcards. She's taking care of that house for her cousin Andy. I can't imagine being a pastor, and I can't imagine them really getting along that well, but they did all right in Denver, and I guess they're making it in Crystal okay."

"That's because Andy's actually in Port Tiffany," said her dad.

"Dad, that wasn't nice."

He sighed. "I know it. I'm just tired of so much of the focus in our lives being on living the perfect Christian example, when deep down we weren't so perfect. And I don't really know Andy. Maybe he's a nice guy. But I'm suspect of all pastors right now."

Jasmine did not respond. She wanted to be careful in this conversation, and let her dad ease in whatever way he could, whatever way was comfortable. She smiled at him and he asked her about her classes. She went through them as discerningly as she could, not being pushy, but waiting for him to bring up the topics that the conversation would actually be about, the reason for his visit. He came because of her questions, her requests, but she would let him take his time. A family is as sick as its secrets, and her future, the future of them all, was about to improve dramatically. *But don't ruin it by being impatient.*

He was so considerate of her; she was not used to that.

"Okay, Jasmine. Now I want you to speak quite frankly to me."

"I'll do my best, Dad."

"I'd like to know the best thing about being away at college, what you're enjoying most, and what is the most stressful thing. Take your time."

"Okay, are you ready? I mean I don't take sides between you and Mom."

"Right. That wouldn't be good. I'll enjoy my steak while you mull it over. And how is your steak?"

"Great, Dad. Truly great. The cafeteria food isn't bad, but this is wonderful."

"Good. Well, you enjoy every bite, and then we'll talk. I'm all ears."

Jasmine did take her time. She was more than half done with her steak before she spoke. "I think I'll surprise you with my answer."

"Surprise me."

"I think they are all the same thing. I think the hardest thing is that I make my own decisions about my own time. If I don't get to the cafeteria on time, I won't eat. If I don't schedule myself and my studies and getting to know some kids, I'll pay a price."

"Wow," said Larry. "Tell me more."

"The *best* thing is, I feel really good when I manage my time right.

It's like, wow, I don't have you or Mom whispering in my ear, making sure I'm eating on time, getting where I need to be. I'm doing it myself, and when it goes well, it feels really good. And that goes for the money management, too. I make my own choices, and see it go well or not so well."

He beamed at her. "Wow. That's great. I'm proud of you. It's been a difficult year for you, and you are handling it well."

That's unusual, compliments from Dad. And he isn't making cracks about Mom. Things are looking up. And he was even generous with lunch. Usually he complains about the cost, the pricey restaurant, and then Mom gets defensive.

"What about you, Dad, how are things going for you?" This wasn't how Jasmine had planned and pictured this conversation, but it was going so unusually well, that it felt wonderful. No strife meant wonderful. Didn't it?

"First, let's talk about dessert. Didn't I see your favorite thing on menu? Tiramasu?!"

They ordered dessert and ate in mostly comfortable silence, but Jasmine got the feeling her dad was holding back something.

Half way through dessert, she said, "This is delicious, Dad. But, let's get back to you. What's going on?"

"For starters, I need to tell you that I am getting married soon."

"Oh. That was fast." What was she supposed to say to that? Was this the honesty that she had wanted, dreamed of, and planned for? No. What was she supposed to say now? Dad, why couldn't you wait a while? What's the matter, Dad, have you been behaving like a teenage boy? Is there a baby on the way?

"Jasmine? Are you okay? Did you hear what I said?" asked her father.

"Yeah, Dad. Sure. I heard everything. I just don't know what to say. What am I supposed to say? Congratulations? Too bad Mom and I weren't good enough for you?"

"Jasmine, would you at least give me a chance?"

"Sure, Dad. A chance for what. Looks like we missed the part where we all got a chance to understand what happened and learn from it before we moved on."

They both went back to eating their desserts. Her dad made an attempt at a joke, which she ignored. They continued in a painful silence.

Finally, they sat, looking at the empty dessert dishes, unable to pretend any longer, unable to manufacture a conversation.

When his phone rang, he ignored it at first, as if he was trying to put something into words, but when the phone rang again, he looked at it, and said, "We need to go outside. I have a surprise for you."

What could it be? The lunch date had felt so good and then had fallen flat. She had so much wanted this to be a time where her dad shared with her what he thought of their family dynamics gone wrong. A time of looking honestly at their lives and the future. Didn't that make sense? That before she could throw herself into her new life, that she would do better to understand the life she just left? Wasn't this the gift her father had intended to give her with this lunch date? What happened to her expectations about how wonderful this was going to be?

Her dad helped her with her jacket and they stepped out into the cool fall air. He had his arm around her, and they walked down the sidewalk to the parking lot with him telling her about his mistakes in college. She laughed, trying to resurrect the good feelings from earlier in their lunch date. She had not seen him this way before, playful and conversational, and the date started to feel wonderful again.

They turned around the corner of the building, and Jasmine saw Tony, her dad's assistant, leaning against a car. He smiled at her and Jasmine's heart melted. What was he doing here? She'd had the biggest crush on him, up until he got married and had twin girls, who were just now walking.

"Are you breaking all the boys' hearts?" asked Tony after he gave her a high five.

"No, not really. They don't even know I exist," she said.

"Oh, come on, I find that hard to believe. Isn't there someone special?"

"There's a special one that I like, but he just doesn't think I'm special."

"Well, we're about to take care of that and his judgment," said her dad.

"What are you talking about?" asked Jasmine.

"Look at this car Tony is leaning on. Literally, you can leave him in the dust."

Tony moved away from the car and Jasmine couldn't believe her eyes.

The vehicle, a small black SUV sparkled in the Colorado sun. It looked all business, like black vehicles do. She looked at her dad, questioning him. He smiled at her and nodded.

"It's yours. All yours. And don't you give anybody a ride that you don't want to, and that means especially boys who don't appreciate you."

"Oh, Dad! It's beautiful!" She walked around it, letting her hand caress it. "This is just unbelievable."

"Like I said, leave anybody stupid enough to not appreciate you *in the dust.*"

Jasmine could not stop her rising excitement — she appreciated the beauty of the car, and knew that this vehicle was about to make her life different. But, also what tugged at her was an uncomfortable feeling that she couldn't put into words; it felt like she was missing something. The excitement pulled her one way, and that other thing, whatever it was, lurked in her mind, seeming to say, "Look here. Look at this more closely. You're missing something."

Jasmine chose not to look at it. Whatever it was would wait. Wouldn't it? How could anyone want her to do anything else than just appreciate this car? And it would make a difference in her college life. She needed a part-time job, and this car would be crucial to that effort.

"Let's get in, you drive, and let's see what this baby can do," said her dad. And so, they did, with Tony in the back. Jasmine got in the front seat, and adjusted the leather seat, the moon roof, and looked at all the bells and whistles. The latest in technology and all hers. She ran her hand over the leather-covered steering wheel.

"You deserve it, kid," said her dad.

"I wish my dad loved me this much," said Tony from the back seat.

Jasmine turned and gave him a look. "As I recall, your dad passed on a number of years ago."

"Right. Are you going to take this baby for a spin or what?"

Jasmine turned the key, listened to the powerful but quiet purr of the engine. She smiled at her dad and Tony, and then she eased out, feeling the automobile's unleashed power, the luxury, as she drove through the parking lot. As they drove by other kids, Jasmine's self-esteem soared. Her dad opened the sunroof and the fresh air enveloped Jasmine, making her move along with exhilaration. What a beautiful car. And the leather smelled new. It was the fragrance of success and assurance that everything will be okay now. The feel of the car blocked everything else out of her mind.

They turned on to the highway and headed east, toward Kansas. The highway stretched before them, flat, straight -- nothing ahead. The vehicle surged forward. Her dad didn't say anything, and Jasmine basked in the wonderfulness of it all. Her dad turned on the radio and the music filled the space with the beat and joy of power. After a while, Larry asked, "Don't you think we ought to turn around? I take it this vehicle meets your approval?"

"Oh, yes. It's wonderful. More than I dreamed I would ever have. It really gives me a sense of self-confidence. What a surprise. I didn't imagine anything like this."

"Like I said, leave those boys behind you. Don't take any guff from anybody. Got that?"

"I do. I'm going to go far with this. This makes a lot of things simpler, and right."

"I've got to get back to Denver. Why don't you fly this thing back to the college?"

Jasmine pulled off the highway and into a truck stop, where they each got a cup of coffee and then they started back. "And don't for a second think that you are allowed one drop of coffee on those car seats," said Jasmine, only half kidding.

"Yes, ma'am," said Tony. She looked at him in the mirror, and they smiled at each other.

She drove back to Colorado Springs feeling empowered about her life. She was only fleetingly aware that they had not talked about the issues that they needed to talk about, but the new car went a long way to making her happy. All those discussions could happen another day. The car, all the respect, and everything about the visit made her happy. And that's all that mattered. Today was a new day, and those other issues, they didn't seem so important now.

∼

Joanne showed Andy around the house, and then fixed him a cup of tea. He smiled at her and waited. He knew she needed to talk.

"I feel like I've been here for years, instead of just a few weeks."

"When God decides we need lessons, He can go pretty fast. Keeping up with him, that's important. Surrendering to it might be a more accurate statement."

"Well, He filled my bucket a little more than I thought I needed."

Andy laughed and waited for her to speak.

"Why are you laughing? You know the story. It's awful and I'm at the center of it. I couldn't be more ashamed, and I feel like I've let you down tremendously. I'm just so grateful the little girl is home with her parents."

"I'm not laughing at you. I'm laughing with you."

"You are not. Don't try to pull that on me. You knew what I micromanager of lives I am, and you were waiting for me to get my lessons. And aren't we all thankful that Clarin and that family, that precious family is safe."

"Sometimes we can't tell people things, they need to go through it themselves, and we need to trust God. Of course, the safety of Clarin was the most important thing. But, do you get that it's a serious thing, to undermine another person's judgment? We all need to practice making decisions, starting when we are young. If we are to make good judgments when we are older, we need to start practicing when we are younger."

"Oh, I get it. And I need to go home, and not just take care of business, like selling a house. I'd like to have a good sit down and talk with Larry and Jasmine. I could really surprise them with owning up to not being so perfect. The subtle stuff I've done to control both — I'm probably only beginning to see how damaging that was."

"You're in a good place. We can only change ourselves."

"That's so easy to say. The truth is I got a postcard from Jasmine. She's thrilled that Larry bought her a car, a brand-new car, and she's enthralled. Hard to compete with that, with open discussions about the past and owning my own mistakes. In Jasmine's eyes, that won't be as much as a new car."

"Sounds like you've learned something! What are you going to do?"

"My ex-husband and I have an agreement that we will list the house in the middle of December. We will have an open house, and I will be in charge of that, making it an event for the holidays. It will sell fast."

"I'm sure you'll do an excellent job. But, what will you do besides that?"

"I'd like to stay here for Thanksgiving. I've been humbled. I'd like a chance to stay, even though your family will be here. Would you let me stay? Would your family mind if I intruded on their holiday? I'll clean up the guest house and stay there."

"They will be fine with that," said Andy. "I can guarantee that this house will be loud, full of loud people, music, and messier than it is right now. You will not be alone anymore."

"I can handle that. I've no other place to go. When I go back to Colorado, to sell the house, I'd like to have that big talk with Jasmine and Larry, but it probably won't happen. I have a feeling it would be wrong to push for it. I want to tell them what has happened here, and how it has affected me, but, I don't know that they will get it. Or believe me."

"That may be true. I personally think you are going to have to white-knuckle a lot of it. You're used to being quiet and having everything organized just so."

"I need to do it, and I would like to be here for Thanksgiving. For me. I need the noise, the new people, and to not be in control. And walk with Jesus at the same time. Although the thought of it scares me to death."

He nodded and then said, "And you need to consider this. After Christmas, we will go back to Port Tiffany. You could come back after Christmas, after finishing up your business in Colorado. If you wanted a place to be, you could come back and stay until summer. It would help me a lot for you to take care of the house until we can come for the summer, and maybe give you a soft place to land."

She got up and went to the window. "I never got a chance to fix the greenhouse up, or that garage guest quarters thing out there. I actually only went into that little apartment once. It was a little scary and dirty, compared to this house." She glanced over her shoulder at Andy. "I'd like to accept your offer."

"Think you can be that far away from your daughter that long?"

"She can handle it. She probably even needs it. And my ex won't miss me at all. I'd like to listen more for the still small voice of God. I think I am not as smart as I thought I was. Obviously. I could do that here."

He didn't reply, and she continued. "Do you think the people of Crystal will accept me after all that's happened? Busybody, *church-lady busybody*, hits town and starts trying to manipulate people, to everyone's detriment. Jasmine used to say I didn't give her room to breathe. I think I'm just starting to understand that. The truth is, I'm rather tired. Managing people's lives makes me tired. I'm getting older. I need to not waste my energy."

"I think you are on your way, making amends, staying here, and working it out. Look for God day by day and things will be fine. I get tired of people wanting to change someone else. You are willing to change, have God change you. That's the way. Not easy trying to be helpful in life but still stay out of people's business."

Joanne stared out the window and gathered her thoughts to reply.

"I want to go back to Colorado, be free of that house, put my stuff in storage, and come back here. For a few months. I want to listen to God, listen to these people, and see what God can do with me. I want to quit telling God and everyone around me what to do. I think all my adult life, I've looked down on people who had a faith that didn't look like mine. But I think about Deet and Tyler, and I don't even know if they are Christians. But I like who they are. I could learn some things from them. They are refreshing to be around. I have no doubt they wouldn't say the same about me."

Andy got up and went to her. He put his arms on her shoulders. "You're making a start. Take one day at a time, remember, you can't change them. If anybody in this town, and that includes Tyler, needs some space from you, then respect that."

"Do you forgive me?" she asked.

"Oh, dear, cousin. Cousin Joanne." He hugged her. "Of course, I forgive you. But the main thing is I'll look forward to your company and seeing how your life goes from here. Be willing to seek God everyday, learn from Him, maybe quite differently than you have been in the past."

"Oh, I get that. I never want to be guilty of ignoring these lessons. It's been so painful. Please don't tell them I said so, but I can kind of see how I've been annoying Jasmine and Larry." She buried her face in his shoulder. "I can see that I haven't been that much fun. I can see that this is how families get destroyed. No big drama, they just disintegrate."

"Good for you for wanting to come back. I'm pretty sure you'll learn as much about yourself in the coming months as you have in the last few weeks."

"That's pretty scary." She looked up at him with a smile. "When did you get so smart?" she asked.

"I've walked the path of humility that you are walking. And the funny thing about it is that I know you are learning that the truth sets you free to have a good day, even today."

Joanne said, "I've noticed that despite my deal, the day looks bright and there is much to be thankful for. It's weird."

"That's often what happens when we quit worrying about what people think of us, and get real dependent on God," said Andy.

The End

ABOUT R.M. ROGERS

Rita reads, writes, walks, drinks coffee, and enjoys people in the Pacific Northwest.

ALSO BY R.M ROGERS

BUILDING OF THE KINGDOM

Book One: Love That House
Book Two: Singing Windows
Book Three: Home of the Bears

Made in the USA
Columbia, SC
11 December 2017